W9-BZA-780

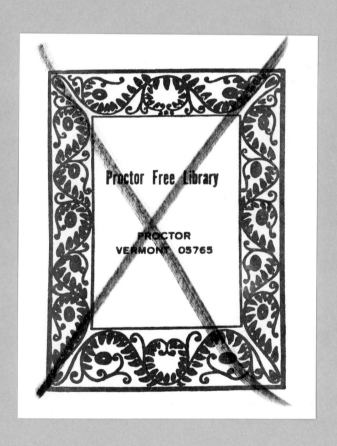

THE
GOLDEN CARP

THE
GOLDEN CARP

AND OTHER TALES FROM VIETNAM

LYNETTE DYER VUONG • MANABU SAITO

LOTHROP, LEE & SHEPARD BOOKS   NEW YORK

First Edition 1 2 3 4 5 6 7 8 9 10

Library of Congress Cataloging in Publication
Vuong, Lynette Dyer, The golden carp, and other tales of Vietnam /
Lynette Vuong ; paintings by Manabu Saito.   p.   cm. Contents: A friend's affection—The ogre's victim—Tears of
Pearl—Third Daughter—Second in command—The golden carp. ISBN 0-688-12514-X 1. Fairy tales—Vietnam. [1. Fairy tales.
2. Folklore—Vietnam.] I. Saito, Manabu C., ill. II. Title. III. Title: Golden carp. PZ8.V889Go 1993 398.21'09597—dc20 92-38208
CIP AC

TO MY SISTER GUIN,

for her encouragement
and for sharing my love of these tales

CONTENTS

INTRODUCTION   9

A FRIEND'S AFFECTION   13

THE OGRE'S VICTIM   29

TEARS OF PEARL   50

THIRD DAUGHTER   69

SECOND IN COMMAND   79

THE GOLDEN CARP   94

AUTHOR'S NOTES   119

PRONUNCIATION OF VIETNAMESE NAMES   126

$\mathcal{I}$NTRODUCTION

$\mathcal{I}$n the spring of 1963, while teaching English as a second language at the Vietnamese-American Association in Saigon, I assigned an advanced group of students to prepare stories to tell to the class. One student, Phạm thị Ngọc-Dung, chose the tale of Lưu Bình and Dương Lễ ("A Friend's Affection") for her presentation. Sensing my interest in the story, a few weeks later Dung presented me with a copy of it that she had found at a local bookstore. This was my introduction, not only to Lưu Bình and Dương Lễ, but to the world of Vietnamese legend.

At about the same time, another student, Chung Lệ-Hoa, invited me to go to a Chinese movie with her. That day I was introduced to my first Asian fairy and fell in love with her. Since we shared an interest in the world of old China and Vietnam, Hoa and I went to see other movies, most of them with English and/or Vietnamese subtitles. On one occasion, however, when there was only the Chinese soundtrack, Hoa, who has both Chinese and Vietnamese ancestry and speaks both languages fluently, acted as my interpreter.

In the years that followed, I returned again and again both to the movies and to my favorite bookstores, buying each new tale or collection as it became available. Folklore had been my special interest since childhood; here was a whole new vein to be mined. Among my favorites were the romantic tales. Some had heroes and heroines like Lưu Bình and Hoa Mộc Lan: ordinary people doing everyday things—in unusual, though not in supernatural, ways. Other heroes and heroines, such as Thạch Sanh and Third Daughter, while they were ordinary people, received help from the fairy world. Still others, such as Châu Nương and Kim Nương, were themselves members of the fairy world who sought, with varying degrees of success, to find a place for themselves among humans. But the common denominator, as in much of folklore the world over, was romance. It has been said that love makes the world go round. Certainly that is true throughout the world of legend, whether the lovers belong to the human or the fairy world.

In retelling these stories, I have used the Vietnamese versions found in Hoàng Trọng Miên's *Việt-Nam Văn-Học Toàn Thư* (The complete literature of Vietnam. Saigon: Văn-Hữu Á Châu Publishing Company, 1959); the series of Vietnamese children's stories written by Tô Lan Chi and illustrated by Lê Trung (Saigon: Minh Đức Publishers, 1962); and by Phi Sơn and Ngân Liên, illustrated by Hoàng Lương (Cholon: Hồng Dân Book Company, 1964–1966); and Nguyễn Duy's *Truyện Cổ Việt-Nam* (Old stories of Vietnam. Saigon: Bốn Phương Publishers, 1940). Much of my understanding of life in old China and Vietnam I owe to the Chinese movies that it was my privilege to see during the years I lived in Saigon: thanks to them I was able to visit this world "in person." I would also like to express special thanks to my husband, who sat through many of the movies with me (when he would rather have been watching an American Western), and for all the questions he has answered and the suggestions he has offered on the written drafts; to Phạm thị Ngọc-Dung and to Chung Lê-Hoa (now Hoa Woo), who first introduced these stories to me; and to LoraBeth Norton, former editor of *Reflection*, who published a version of "A Friend's Affection" in that magazine's September–October 1981 issue.

A FRIEND'S AFFECTION

Faint with hunger, Luu Binh reached into his pocket. He turned the coin over and over in his hand. The smell of freshly fried fish tantalized him, tortured him, as he hesitated outside the door of the restaurant. Should he eat now or save his last coin for dinner tonight?

The sound of cheers drowned out the rumbling of his stomach. A parade was coming down the road. Soldiers in red hats and tunics, blue sashes knotted about their waists, stepped in time to the trot of a magnificent white horse. The rider sat under a parasol, dressed in fine brocade and a golden cap. He must be a newly appointed mandarin. The thought grated like the taste of bitter melon. He, too, would have passed the imperial exam if he had listened to his friend

Duong Le and attended to his studies instead of wasting his time and money at the wineshops and teahouses.

He squinted as the horse drew nearer. It was Duong Le under all that finery! How different he had looked the night Luu Binh had first seen him, crouching under an open window, struggling in the dismal light to make out the characters in his book. He had gone without lunch for a month in order to buy it. Luu Binh had taken Duong Le home with him. For the next two years he had lived with Luu Binh's family like a son and a brother, eating with them from one tray, studying with Luu Binh by the light of one lamp.

That had been when Luu Binh's father was still alive, before Luu Binh had squandered his inheritance—the inheritance that had seemed inexhaustible in the beginning. How fine he had looked then in his perfectly cut robes of the best silks. He had been the favorite of all the girls, the life of every party. What would Duong Le say if he could see him now in his patched shirt and tattered pants?

But Duong Le knew what it was to be poor. He would not scorn his friend just because Luu Binh had fallen on hard times. Duong Le would be eager to help, now that their positions were reversed.

The soldiers disappeared around a bend in the road. Luu Binh dashed after the bright red tunics. He overtook them just as they turned into the mayor's residence. Imagine, his old friend being appointed mayor! There he stood on the steps of his new home. Luu Binh followed the last of the soldiers into the courtyard and hurried toward the mansion.

Luu Binh saw a glimmer of shocked recognition in Duong Le's eyes before Duong Le turned away and started toward the door.

Luu Binh rushed up the steps after him. "Duong Le! Don't you remember me?"

A hand gripped Luu Binh's shoulder as Duong Le glanced at the guards and shook his head. "I don't know the man. I've never seen him before."

"Never seen me before!" Luu Binh cried. "Don't you recognize me? I'm your old friend Luu Binh in spite of these rags. Now I am the one who needs your help."

Duong Le clucked sympathetically. "The poor man must be mad with hunger. Guards, take him back to the kitchen and see that he gets something to eat."

"To the kitchen! Is that where you ate when you sat in your patched, dingy robes at my table?" Luu Binh shouted over his shoulder as the guards dragged him away. "I recognize you well enough, strange as you look in your fine clothes. How is it you don't know me in my rags? Has the gold of your mandarin cap blinded your eyes?"

Too weak to resist any longer, he let the soldiers lead him around the back to a building surrounded by coconut palms.

The cook glanced up as the guards shoved Luu Binh through the door. "Is this the beggar His Excellency wants fed?" he asked. He slapped a bowl of rice and a raw eggplant onto a tray and plunked it down on a mat in one corner of the room.

Luu Binh slumped to the floor, his face to the wall. He rubbed his sleeve against his eyes. Was this all his "friend" could spare him, a bowl of rice and one measly eggplant, while he feasted inside his mansion? Had anyone ever seen such ingratitude? Never would Luu Binh have believed that Duong Le could be so changed by his good fortune.

Luu Binh dipped the last bite of eggplant into the fish sauce and shoved it into his mouth with the remaining grains of rice. He set down the bowl and chopsticks and rose to his feet. Avoiding the cook's eyes, he hurried to the door and rushed across the courtyard, through the gate, out into the street. Never would he return to that house! He would starve to death first.

The sun beat down on Luu Binh's head as he walked through the town. He trudged on, down one road, then another, not caring which one he took. Just putting one foot in front of the other was an effort. He would rest a few moments under the tree up ahead while he decided how to spend his last copper. He sank down, leaning his aching back against the trunk, and closed his eyes.

"Coconut juice. Fresh coconut juice."

The singsong cry jolted him awake. A girl was coming down the road, two baskets suspended from the pole on her shoulder. She stopped as she reached the tree.

"Would you like some coconut juice?" she asked. "There's nothing better when you're hot and tired."

Without waiting for a reply, she raised the lid of her basket and took out a coconut. She chopped off its top; then, upending it over a bowl from the other basket, she poured out the juice.

Luu Binh reached into his pocket. He might as well quench his thirst. One copper would hardly be enough for dinner anyway.

But she shook her head. "Keep your money. I offered you the drink; you didn't ask for it." She sat down across from him, next to her baskets. "Do you have much farther to go?"

Luu Binh gave a bitter laugh. "If you want to know the truth, I have nowhere to go."

She frowned thoughtfully. "There's an abandoned house down the road a way. It's nothing fancy, but it'd be better than sleeping out-of-doors."

"It's kind of you to tell me about it." Not that it matters, he mumbled to himself. "I might look for it later."

"It must be dusty. I'll come by tomorrow morning and sweep it for you. That is, if you wouldn't mind."

"I wouldn't mind." He smiled in spite of himself, then slumped back into glumness. "Though why you should bother, I can't imagine. No one else would," he added, more to himself than to her, "not even my best friend."

"Your best friend?" She raised her eyebrows.

Before he knew it, he had poured out the whole story. "That's how he treats me"— he spat out the words— "after all I did for him. The

books he studied from, the ink he wrote with, the oil for his lamp—
they were all bought with money I gave him. Gave, and never asked
to be repaid. So how does he treat me now? Like a beggar."

She nodded slowly. "Such are the ways of the world. But forget
his ingratitude. It's your future you must be concerned about."

"What future?" He shrugged. "Of course I've brought it all on
myself. That's probably why Duong Le wants nothing to do with
me. He used to tell me that pursuing moonlight and flowers would
bring me sorrow. But I wouldn't listen. I thought my father's name
and money were all I needed. I wasn't like Duong Le, with nothing
but my lamp and books to ensure my future. Or so I thought then."
He leaned back against the tree, sighing.

"There'll be another exam three years from now," Chau Long
reminded him. "If you apply yourself, there's no reason why you,
too, shouldn't be successful." Her eyes probed his. "Promise me that
you will. When I come tomorrow morning, I'll bring some books
with me. My brother has finished his studies and doesn't need them
anymore." She rose, lifting the pole onto her shoulder. "I must go if
I intend to sell the rest of these coconuts before nightfall."

He watched her walk away, his mind in a whirl. Would she really come, as she had promised? Or was it some kind of joke? Her name was Chau Long, she had told him. She hadn't asked for his name.

Luu Binh turned over as the morning sun hit his face. The house was just down the road, as Chau Long had said. At least that much of what she had told him was true.

Someone was knocking on the door. With a yawn he pulled himself to his feet and went to answer it.

Chau Long smiled as she stepped inside. "Did you sleep well last night?" she asked him. "You look rested." She eased the pole off her shoulder and set down her baskets, then bent to untie the mat and broom secured to the pole.

"There's breakfast in one of the baskets." Chau Long picked up the broom and set to work as she talked. "And some clothes. My brother sent them to you along with the books. We had a lamp that we weren't using; so he told me to bring that, too." She swept off the table, a rude piece of furniture the previous occupant had left behind, and shoved it over toward the window.

Luu Binh squatted next to the baskets, lifting out the books one by one. She had brought ink and brushes and writing paper as well.

That strangers should do so much for him overwhelmed him. Their kindness made Duong Le's ingratitude even more galling.

Chau Long stood the broom in the corner. "Doesn't that look better?" She smiled as she gazed about the room. "I'll be going now, but I'll be back with dinner for you."

"Chau Long, it's most kind of you. But I can't let you do all this for me. I have no way to repay you."

"Don't worry about repaying me." She reached into her pocket and took out a roll of bright red paper. "A merchant I know needs someone to write good-luck verses. I'll take them to him when you're finished. I'm sure I can find plenty of such work for you." She left then.

Luu Binh went over to the table. All morning he sat in front of his books, chanting the passages to memorize them. In the afternoon he filled strip after strip of the red paper with careful strokes, then laid each one aside to dry. When he had finished, he took up the books again. His back ached from the long hours of sitting, but he ignored the pain.

Toward the end of the afternoon, Chau Long returned with food and a charcoal stove to cook dinner for him. Luu Binh's eyes strayed from his books to watch her as she worked. She moved with grace, even in performing the simplest chores. The day before, he hadn't noticed how lovely she was. With the proper dress she would fit in the most select society.

"You've stopped reading." She turned from the stove and noticed his gaze on her. "Do go on. I was listening."

Luu Binh looked down at his book again and continued his chanting. The lesson was more interesting when she was there to hear it.

Days passed and weeks grew into months as Luu Binh pursued his studies. Every morning on her way to market Chau Long came to prepare his breakfast and to sweep the house. She always had a word of encouragement for him. In the evenings she returned to cook his dinner, to wash his clothes, and to ask him how the day had gone. The road to success was so wearisome that he was often tempted to abandon his studies. But how could he admit such thoughts to Chau Long? She believed in him, and she was looking forward to the day he would set off for the capital to take his exam. If only she could be with him always. The hours she spent with him seemed so short, and the time he waited for her return so lengthy.

"Chau Long," he said to her one day, "will you marry me?"

He saw her smile before she turned and her long hair hid her face. "You must not think of that now," she replied softly. "You must keep your mind free for your studies. When you return from the exam, I will be waiting."

A year passed and then another; whenever Luu Binh repeated his question, her answer was the same. Luu Binh doubled his efforts as the time for the exam drew nearer. He could not fail, not after all Chau Long had done for him. He must return to her in triumph.

At last the day came. Luu Binh stood in front of the house. Tears gathered in his eyes as he gazed down at Chau Long. "Promise me you'll be here when I return," he said. "Promise you will wait for me."

She smiled up at him through wet lashes. "I'll be waiting. And my heart will be glowing as brightly as the golden cap you will be wearing."

"If I come home with that cap on my head it will be thanks to you." He held her hands in his, pressing them as he spoke. He longed to take her in his arms, but he dared not. "Chau Long, I love you," he whispered. "Each day we are separated will be a hundred winters."

"Yes, but Heaven will send spring again." She eased her fingers from his. "The road is long, and the sun is high. You must be on your way."

He turned and started down the road that wound toward the capital, looking back every few feet to see Chau Long still standing there, her arm raised in farewell. At last she was only a speck floating on the surface of his tears. Finally he could no longer distinguish even the house against the horizon.

Day after day he followed the road, from one village to another, stopping each night to seek a meal and lodging at a pagoda along the way. Each morning he rolled up his bedding, slung it onto his back, and continued his journey, until the walls of the capital rose before him. Inside the city, he joined the other candidates who had come to take the exam. When the results were announced, Luu Binh's name headed the list. He stood before the king to receive the brocade robe and gold cap of his new rank and his appointment as district chief.

Dressed in his finery, Luu Binh rode back to his hometown, escorted by an honor guard who called out his accomplishments for all to hear. They were leading him to the mayor's mansion to be greeted and congratulated by the town officials. How he would enjoy the sight of Duong Le's face when Duong Le saw him ride up on a white horse! No doubt Duong Le's memory would be better today than it had been three years ago.

But even sweeter was the thought of seeing Chau Long again. He longed to urge the horse into a gallop, but the guards led him onward at their own pace.

At last they reached the house. Luu Binh swung out of his saddle and bounded to the door, thrusting it open.

"Chau Long," he called. "Your mandarin is home—in his red brocade and gold cap."

The curtains were drawn, and dust covered the table. Nothing answered his calls but the echoes of his own voice, mocking him. Deep in his heart he could feel tears, but he was too numb even to weep.

He stumbled out of the house and pulled himself onto his horse like a body without its spirit. The parade had become a funeral procession, and he the corpse. Only as the entourage halted before the mayor's mansion, as he remembered the shame he had suffered there three years before, did he feel a stab of life.

Luu Binh's heart swelled with anger at the smile of welcome on Duong Le's face. "It seems you know me today, Duong Le? Perhaps this gold cap I'm wearing has sparked your memory. Without me you would never have reached the position you're in today. But I have succeeded on my own, no thanks to you." He swung his horse toward the gate. "Now that you've seen me, I'll be going. Never will I eat another meal under your roof."

Duong Le grasped the reins to stop him. "My friend and my brother, don't go until you have heard me out. It's true that you made it possible for me to become what I am today. Then wasn't I obligated to do the same for you? But if I had taken you in, wouldn't you have continued your carefree ways? Would you be wearing that gold cap today if I had given you then what you sought from me? I had to devise a plan that would help you, not for one day only, but for the rest of your life."

"What are you talking about? What did you do for me except insult me and treat me like a beggar and then drive me from your door?" Luu Binh jerked at the reins. "For all you cared, I could have starved to death. And I would have if Heaven had not sent one far better than you to my rescue."

"Luu Binh. Look behind you."

A girl was coming down the steps, dressed in red, wearing a golden bridal crown. His heart beat faster. It was Chau Long!

"Won't you come in now?" Duong Le was saying. "The feast I've prepared in your honor is ready, and your bride is waiting. Chau Long is my sister. I sent her after you that day to watch out for you and to encourage you until you, too, became a success. Now we will celebrate not only your new position but your wedding as well."

Duong Le dropped the reins as Luu Binh, tears of joy in his eyes, climbed down from his horse and embraced his old friend—now his brother.

THE OGRE'S VICTIM

*L*y Thong eased the pole off his shoulder and, laying his vegetable baskets on the ground, sank down under the tree beside them. It was getting dark, and he ought not to be lingering in the forest. Not that it made any difference now, with what faced him tomorrow. He lifted the end of the towel around his neck and wiped the sweat from his forehead. If only it were some horrible nightmare and he could wake to find it gone. He felt in his pocket for the roll of paper the king's soldier had shoved into his hand that afternoon as he sat in the marketplace selling his vegetables. No, he hadn't dreamed it; it was still there. The ogre that had been terrorizing the countryside for the past several years had to be appeased again. And this time it was his family's turn to supply the victim. That meant him, of course, since there were only he and his aged mother.

The snapping of a twig jerked him back to the present. A tiger was about to pounce on him. He sprang to his feet, but it was too late. The tiger was upon him; he could feel its claws tearing his back. Then, just as suddenly, the tiger's body went limp. Ly Thong crawled out from under it and gazed up at the tall, broad-shouldered young man standing beside him.

"Are you all right?" the man asked him.

Ly Thong gaped from the tiger sprawled on the ground to the ax in the young man's hand. The man was as handsome as a prince, though he wore nothing but a ragged loincloth wrapped around his hips.

"How can I ever thank you? You saved my life!" Ly Thong finally managed to gasp. "Do you live nearby—you and your family?" he added, as a plan began to form in his mind.

Thach Sanh bent to pick up the bundle of wood he had dropped. "I have a hut on the edge of the forest," he answered. "I live alone now that my parents are gone."

"I, too, am alone except for my mother." He put his arm around the young man's back. "Come live with us. We will be brothers."

Ly Thong slipped his shoulder under the pole once again, and the two continued on together. Perhaps his situation was not hopeless after all. If he played it right, he might yet escape the horrible fate that awaited him. What a stroke of luck that this strong, handsome fellow had come into his life.

As the first rays of sunlight slanted through the window, Ly Thong opened his eyes. He propped himself on his elbow and glanced at the handsome face on the mat next to him. What big muscles Thach Sanh had, Ly Thong thought as he rolled up his mat and shoved it into the corner. It was a shame, really. Someone with his strength would have been useful around the farm.

His mother was preparing breakfast when he opened the door and stepped into the other room. Ly Thong hurried to help her, reminding her in whispers of the plan they had worked out the night before.

The door opened, and Thach Sanh joined them.

"You're just in time for breakfast," Ly Thong greeted him, indicating the place set for him on the mat. "Did you sleep well last night?"

Thach Sanh smiled, a warm smile that almost made Ly Thong

lower his eyes in shame. "Yes, very well, thank you, brother." He held out both hands politely to receive the generous serving of rice and vegetables that Ly Thong's mother had scooped into his bowl.

Ly Thong glanced at his mother, his chopsticks hovering over his rice bowl. "I'll take the greens to market first thing tomorrow morning," he said as he picked up a mouthful. "That is, if they're not too wilted by then."

His mother frowned. "You don't think you could take them today and do the work at the shrine tomorrow?"

Ly Thong shook his head. "The king plans to visit the shrine tomorrow. If he finds it in disorder, it could go hard with us." Out of the corner of his eye he noticed Thach Sanh's gaze turn toward him with concern.

"Is there anything I can do to help?" Thach Sanh asked him.

"It's my turn to sweep out the king's shrine and make sure everything's in order before his next visit," Ly Thong explained with a sigh. "But Mother forgot about my having to go today and has picked a lot of greens for me to sell."

Thach Sanh laid a hand on his arm. "You take the greens to market. I'll go and sweep out the shrine."

"I couldn't let you do that!" Ly Thong twisted his face into a frown. "You have your own work to do."

"I can sell my wood tomorrow just as well as today." Thach Sanh finished his breakfast and, shouldering his ax, started toward the door. "What are brothers for if not to help each other?"

Ly Thong felt a twinge of guilt as the door closed behind him, but he thrust it away. After all, Thach Sanh was an orphan. His death would be no loss to anyone but himself. But who would support Ly Thong's aged mother if *he* were devoured by the ogre?

Thach Sanh whistled to himself as he swung down the road. He hadn't felt so lighthearted in years. How good to know he was no longer alone in the world! He smiled, thinking back on the welcome Ly Thong's mother had given him the night before. He hadn't had food like that since his own mother died. How generous they both were to him. Really, he hadn't done anything that anyone in his position wouldn't have done. Who wouldn't save a person's life if he had the chance?

As he rounded a bend in the road he saw a grove in the distance. A red roof peeked out from among the trees.

Suddenly a bloodcurdling roar came from the grove. A giant hand with long, pointed claws swept aside the foliage, revealing a terrifying figure. An ogre, his huge body as hairy as an ape's, was walking toward Thach Sanh, upright like a man. Two sharp horns grew from the top of his head; and his bloodshot eyes, as round as fish-sauce bowls, gleamed at Thach Sanh while his tongue swished back and forth across tusks that jutted from each side of his mouth. With a bellow that shook the treetops he rushed at Thach Sanh, grabbing for him with his claws. Thach Sanh dodged and swung at him with his ax, then leapt back when he felt the ogre's hot breath on his face. Great flames poured from the ogre's nostrils, singeing Thach Sanh's hair and setting fire to the tree behind him.

Thach Sanh ducked behind the tree and swung his ax at it. He strained every muscle to catch the tree as it fell. Then, lifting it high, he shoved the burning leaves into the ogre's face. The ogre's roars weakened to fits of coughing; he groped through the smoke and leaves, lunging for his assailant. Thach Sanh drove the ax into his body. The ogre struck the ground like a bolt of lightning, knocking

down all the trees in his path. Cautiously Thach Sanh crept up to him and chopped off his head. Then he walked on through the trees to sweep the shrine, as he had promised.

Thach Sanh trudged through the night, his ax in one hand, the ogre's head in the other. He hoped Ly Thong and his mother weren't waiting supper for him.

He laid the head down and rapped on the door, but there was no answer. He knocked again. Perhaps they were asleep. Well, no matter. He'd go back to his old hut for tonight.

Then he heard Ly Thong's voice calling, "Who's there?"

"It's Thach Sanh," he answered. "I'm home."

The door opened a crack, and Ly Thong peered out anxiously. The door inched open a bit further. Ly Thong stared at him again. Then he saw the head in Thach Sanh's hand, and his eyes gleamed. "Oh, it's you, brother!" He threw open the door. "Come in, come in. Don't stand out there holding that head like that. What if someone should see you?"

Thach Sanh stared as his friend pushed the door shut and bolted it fast. "What's the matter, brother?" he demanded.

"Why, that head!" Ly Thong cried. "Don't you know that's the king's ogre, the special guard who watches over the shrine? But how could you have known?" He cupped his hand under his chin and sighed. "It's all my fault. I should have gone myself instead of sending you. The ogre knows me and wouldn't have attacked me." He laid a hand on Thach Sanh's arm. "But don't worry. I'll go to the king and explain what happened. He just might forgive us."

Thach Sanh bowed his head, overcome by his friend's generosity; but he knew he could not accept it. "I'm the one who made the mistake," he argued, "and I should be the one to pay for it. I won't have you going in my place."

"Now, wait a minute," Ly Thong objected. "Remember what you said this morning, that brothers are to help each other?" He picked up the ogre's head and set it down in the corner. "Now is my chance to prove that I, too, know a brother's duty."

Ly Thong could hardly contain his excitement as he set off the next morning for the king's court. Only the day before yesterday, he had thought his life was finished. But his death sentence had turned out to be the beginning of his good fortune. Of course, in a way he owed it all to Thach Sanh. On the other hand, it had been his own quick thinking that had made it possible. Even so, it was rather a shame to take advantage of Thach Sanh in this way. But then, if you thought about it sensibly, what earthly good would such a simpleminded fellow have for the wealth and position that would soon be Ly Thong's?

The gates of the palace lay just ahead. Ly Thong smirked at the amazed faces of the guards as they escorted him inside to the throne room. How the courtiers gaped as he entered! He strode to the throne and laid the ogre's head before the king.

King and courtiers cheered with one voice as he told the grand tale he had rehearsed along the road. "For seven years this ogre has ravaged our country," the king declared when he finished. "Till now no one has dared to challenge him. Make this brave man the commander of my army."

Ly Thong smiled to himself as the symbols of his new rank were placed on him. How important he looked in his winged cap and his fine robe embroidered with dragons. Things were working out even better than he had dreamed—just so long as Thach Sanh never found out.

ⴲ   ⴲ   ⴲ

Day after day Thach Sanh waited for Ly Thong to return. But weeks passed, and no word came. Perhaps the king had thrown his friend into prison. If only there were some way he could help. But he had promised Ly Thong he would stay and take care of his mother until he got back. It was the least he could do after all their kindness to him.

Thach Sanh swung his ax again, chopping off the branches of the tree he had just felled. So far he had little to show for his morning's work. It was hard to keep his mind on his job, worried as he was about Ly Thong.

A swooshing sound filled the air, and the sky above him darkened. A gigantic hawk flew overhead, a girl clasped in its talons. Thach Sanh raised his ax and flung it at the bird, striking one of its wings. The bird spun in the air, reeling toward the ground as Thach Sanh ran after it, retrieving his ax on the way.

"Thach Sanh! Thach Sanh, wait!"

Thach Sanh wheeled around. Ly Thong was running toward him, surrounded by a company of soldiers.

"Brother!" Thach Sanh exclaimed. "Thank Heaven you're safe! I was so worried when you didn't come home." Then he remembered the girl. "Did you see that hawk just now—"

Ly Thong clasped Thach Sanh's arm, pulling him back. "Yes, it has the Princess Huynh Nga. It swooped down on her as she was walking in the garden. The king ordered me to rescue her. If I do, he's promised to forgive me for the ogre's death. But if not—" He broke off, drawing his index finger across his neck.

"There's no time to lose," Thach Sanh cried, rushing forward. "The hawk is wounded. We must follow its trail until we find the princess."

The fresh blood led them through the forest till they saw the hawk lying ahead of them outside the entrance to a cave. The princess was still caught fast in its talons. Thach Sanh felt his heart quicken as she turned toward him, her lovely phoenix eyes pleading for his help. But before he could reach her, a giant python slithered out of the cave, wound itself around the princess, and pulling her away from the hawk, crawled back inside.

Struck dumb with terror, Huynh Nga gasped for breath as the python's coils tightened around her. Then she saw shadows moving toward her. The man in the lead, his face a blend of strength and gentleness, brought hope to her heart. His ax descended; she felt the coils loosen. Suddenly she was free, as the python turned from her to wrap itself around its assailant. Another man, who had been standing close to the wall, now leapt forward to grab her hand and hurry her toward the exit. She gazed back at the brave hero who was still battling the evil serpent. Why were they leaving him? She tried to protest, but no sound came—only tears, running down her cheeks.

Thach Sanh struggled in the python's grip. Again and again he pounded the blade of his ax against its skin. Finally its coils began to loosen, the snake to weaken. He pulled himself from the coils one by one, sighing with relief when at last the python lay lifeless at his feet. Now the princess was safe, and so was Ly Thong.

He turned, gazing around him in dismay. He was alone, and the cave was even darker than before. He groped toward the exit. But the mouth of the cave had been blocked with earth and stones. Though he swung his ax again and again, the blade was useless against the huge rocks. No doubt the soldiers had been afraid the python would escape and had forgotten that he was still in the cave. But what had happened to Ly Thong that he had not noticed his plight and been able to stop them?

Suddenly he froze. He had heard a groan deep inside the cave. Thach Sanh turned and made his way into the interior, following the sound of the cries as they grew louder and louder.

He stopped short before a brass cage. In the near darkness he made out the form of a man standing inside. Raising his ax, Thach Sanh struck the bars with all his might, until he had cut an opening large enough to crawl through.

"How can I ever repay you!" the man exclaimed as soon as he was free. "I am the son of the Dragon King of the Waters. The evil python kidnapped me and held me prisoner in this cage. He put me in a trance so that I could not move or even cry out, but you broke the spell by destroying him. Come, I will take you to my father. I know he will want to reward you."

What an adventure, to visit the Dragon King's palace under the sea! But how could he think of his own pleasure with Ly Thong's fate still undecided? "Forgive me, sir," Thach Sanh said, "but I must go to the palace. My brother's life is still in danger, and he may need me."

"Very well," the prince agreed. "But I can't let you go without some reward." He reached into the cage and lifted out an object.

"Take this guitar," he said, placing it in Thach Sanh's hands. "May it someday bring you good fortune."

The prince led Thach Sanh to an opening at the other end of the cave, and the two bade each other farewell.

Ly Thong lay against the silk pillows, reliving the day's excitement. His pulse raced, remembering how he had brought Huynh Nga back to her father. With one arm around his daughter, the king had embraced Ly Thong with the other and declared him chief mandarin of his court. A cap of the highest rank was placed on his head, and a feast prepared in his honor. Tomorrow his marriage to the princess would be celebrated, for the king had promised her hand to the one who brought her back safely. It was a good thing Thach Sanh was permanently out of the way, now that Ly Thong wouldn't be needing him anymore. He had seen the way Thach Sanh and Huynh Nga looked at each other in the cave.

A knock sounded at the door, and a servant stepped in. "Sir, your brother is here to see you," he said.

"My brother!" Ly Thong cried. He quickly rearranged his face into a smile as Thach Sanh entered. The two clasped each other's arms in welcome. "It's so good to see you," Ly Thong exclaimed. "You've come at just the right time. I was lying here wondering how I would get some money to my mother." He stopped. "But what am I thinking of? You must be tired after your long journey, and here I am, asking you—"

"Of course I'll go," Thach Sanh interrupted him, clapping his shoulder warmly. "I'll leave at once. She's been worried about you, too. It'll set her mind at rest to know you're safe."

Ly Thong went to the shelf and took down the two bags of gold that the king had entrusted to him that afternoon. He stood holding them for a moment, hesitating. It was a shame to lose both of them. But that was a foolish way to look at it. Actually it was more like an investment. He placed the bags in Thach Sanh's hands and let him out by a back gate.

Thach Sanh set down the bags of gold and pressed his shoulders against a tree to relieve the ache in his back. He hadn't imagined two bags of gold could be so heavy. With a sigh, he adjusted his ax and guitar on his shoulder, then bent to pick up the bags again.

A flash of light jerked him to an upright position. Soldiers surrounded him, their torches held high, their swords unsheathed. One wrenched the bags from his hands while others grabbed him and tied his wrists.

"A brave fellow," one said with a guffaw. "Imagine, daring to steal the king's gold!"

Another snickered. "Let's see how brave he is tomorrow, when he meets the executioner."

"Ly Thong gave me the money," Thach Sanh tried to explain. "I was taking it to his mother."

The soldier next to him dug the hilt of his sword into Thach Sanh's back, prodding him forward. "It's not enough to steal? You must slander the king's son-in-law as well?" He turned to the others. "Come on, let's get this worthless fellow into his cell. We want to be ready for the wedding in the morning."

Their words tumbled around in Thach Sanh's brain as he tried to make sense of them. What did they mean, the king's son-in-law? Had such good fortune come to Ly Thong? Was it the beautiful Huynh Nga he was marrying? A sick feeling stole over him. But of course it was foolish. He could never have hoped to win her anyway, he whose only possessions were his ax, his guitar, and one ragged loincloth. How happy Ly Thong must be. But in all the excitement, would he hear what had happened to his friend soon enough to save him?

The soldiers had stopped in front of a heavy iron door near the palace. The hinges creaked as they drew it open. Thach Sanh felt a shove and fell forward onto the grimy, tattered matting that lay on the floor. Something struck his leg. He turned to see his guitar lying beside him.

"We'll keep the ax and the gold," one of the soldiers was saying as he shut the gate and leered in through the bars. "But you can have the guitar. Play us a sad song or two to take your mind off your troubles."

Huynh Nga sat by her window, staring down at the garden. Tears dampened the red brocade of her wedding dress. Ever since she had felt the hawk's talons lifting her into the sky, not a sound had passed her lips. In vain she had tried to scream for help, and in vain she had struggled to tell her father what had happened the day before. The doctors said that her fright had taken her voice away. Unless it came back soon, she would have to marry that treacherous schemer, Ly

Thong. If only she could tell her father the truth about the brave, handsome hero who had rescued her and how Ly Thong had sealed him up alive in the cave. If only someone could be sent to save him and she could marry him instead. She opened her mouth, coughing and choking, straining to force words from her throat, but no sound came.

The door opened. It must be her attendants come to escort her. She pressed her sleeve to her cheeks, brushed the bead veil over her face, and rose to her feet.

Guests filled the huge pavilion. Through the strands of beads Huynh Nga could see her father at the far end. Ly Thong stood beside him, dressed in a robe of deep blue brocaded with golden dragons. It should have been pythons, she thought to herself. The dragon was too noble a symbol to be worn by such a rascal.

Suddenly she heard music—sweet melancholy strains, not from the flutes and mandolins in the pavilion, but wafted in through the open windows. Tears flowed down Huynh Nga's cheeks as she listened. It seemed that whoever plucked the strings knew the ache in her heart and was telling it all on his guitar. A sob rose in her throat, and a low cry escaped her lips. Then she was weeping as if her heart would break.

Her father's arms were around her. "My precious one, what is it?" he demanded.

"Bring me the guitar player. I must hear him again."

The guests gaped in astonishment as Thach Sanh entered the room, guitar in hand. With a gasp of terror Ly Thong edged toward the door.

"Grab that man!" Huynh Nga cried, brushing the beads from her face. "Don't let Ly Thong escape." She stepped to Thach Sanh's side and led him toward her father. "This is the man who saved my life. This is my rightful bridegroom." She told the story for everyone to hear.

Ly Thong threw himself at Thach Sanh's feet as she finished. "Forgive me, brother," he begged. "I have done nothing but evil to you, and you have repaid me with nothing but good, from the day I sent you to be devoured by the ogre and then told the king that I was the one who destroyed him."

"Enough!" the king cried. He motioned to the guards. "Take off his robe and cap and place them on Thach Sanh, my son and the heir to my throne." He cast a look of contempt at Ly Thong, who still lay sniveling before them. "As for this wretch, take him out of my sight and execute him at once."

But Thach Sanh stepped to Ly Thong's side and lifted him to his feet. "Your Majesty, pardon him," he pleaded. "Even though he has wronged me, he is still my brother. And he has an aged mother to support. Let him go back to her for my sake."

The king nodded reluctantly as the guards placed the blue robe around Thach Sanh's shoulders and pressed the winged cap onto his head. "Then let Heaven decide Ly Thong's punishment. The Thunder Spirit will not leave such a scoundrel unscathed for long. But enough of this. It's my daughter's wedding day." He motioned to the mandolin players and the flutists. "Let's have music," he commanded. "It is time to celebrate."

Huynh Nga raised her eyes to Thach Sanh and gave him a smile that sent his heart racing with joy. Then, with a shake of her head, the bead veil fell, covering her face once more.

$\mathcal{T}$EARS OF $\mathcal{P}$EARL

$\mathcal{T}$he waves tossed the boat to and fro like a piece of driftwood. The wind tore at the sails, ripping them from the masts. Canh Sinh looked out at the sea in concern.

"Head for land," he shouted to his sailors.

The rain beat down, blinding them. With all the effort they could muster, the men pulled at their oars. At last they felt a thud as the boat contacted land. They threw the anchor down, securing it quickly.

Canh Sinh stepped from the boat, sighing in relief. The ship was intact and none of his goods had been lost. He looked around him. The beach stretched before him, barren and deserted, with no sign of human habitation. He started. Something had moved on the rocks

in the distance. He looked again. It was white, and the wind caught it and blew it about like a sail.

As he came nearer he saw a girl sitting on the rock, her head bent, her face hidden from view. She lifted her head as he approached; the wind howled around them as they gazed at each other.

"Where did you come from?" Canh Sinh finally asked her. "Why are you here all alone?"

"I don't know where to go. The people I was looking for are gone."

"Whom were you looking for, in this deserted place?"

"Before my aunt died, she sent me to her native village. But when I arrived, I found nothing but sand and rocks."

The girl was shivering with cold. Canh Sinh glanced around him at the desolate terrain.

"Come aboard my ship," he invited her. "We can wait out the storm there. My name is Canh Sinh," he added when she hesitated. "I'm a merchant."

She stood up. "My name is Chau Nuong."

He helped her down from the rocks. Together the two hurried to shelter.

All day the storm beat against the sides of their ship, but they were safe within and their anchor secure. The next morning, the storm had passed. A light breeze lapped the waves against the shore. Canh Sinh gave orders to lift anchor and to adjust the sails for their homeward course.

He and Chau Nuong stood at the rail, looking out at the sea as they sped along its surface.

"I love the sea," Canh Sinh exclaimed suddenly. "Even though I know its cruelty, I can't help loving it on days like this."

Chau Nuong looked up at him, a new tenderness in her eyes. "I understand," she said softly. "I, too, love the sea. It will always be a part of me."

"If you love the sea, you would love my home. I live on a hill, but my garden runs straight down to the shore. There are walls on three sides; the fourth wall is the sea." He paused, admiring the long black hair hanging over her shoulders. "Chau Nuong, what are your plans for the future?"

"I have no plans."

"My house is large. Come and stay with me. I would like to ask you to be my wife," he went on when she started to protest, "but I'm a man of honor and would not attach conditions to my hospitality. I wouldn't want you to marry me out of a sense of obligation. I hope someday you will be my wife, but now I'm asking you only to be my guest."

"Thank you, Canh Sinh." She gazed at the water, her hair hiding her face from view. "I appreciate what you have just said, and I'll accept your invitation on one condition: that you think of me only in terms of friendship and not of love. I can't bear the thought of hurting you by letting you think there could ever be a marriage between us."

He laughed softly. "It's too early to talk of marriage. I'm satisfied that you're willing to be my friend. Friendship can deepen into love and love into marriage."

She shook her head, still staring at the waves. "Perhaps, but for us it could never be."

"Look, over there in the distance!" he cried, pointing. "There's my house on the top of the hill."

Anticipation filled them both as the ship neared the shore. Even from the boat Chau Nuong could see the beauty of the garden, and through it she glimpsed the soul of the man who had planned it.

Canh Sinh helped her from the ship. Together they walked across the white sand, through the rock garden, and over the bridge that spanned the lotus pond. Butterflies flitted through the blossoming trees.

"It's beautiful, all so beautiful!" Chau Nuong cried in ecstasy. "I never imagined. Everything's so different in my country."

"Tell me about your country."

She hesitated. "Someday I'll tell you about it. Please don't ask me now."

"Of course not. I understand."

The hours passed like a dream. Days flowed into weeks, and weeks into months. The beauty around them filled their mornings, their afternoons, and their evenings. Canh Sinh was content to wait for Chau Nuong's love, and Chau Nuong with gentle determination kept their friendship platonic.

The day came for another of Canh Sinh's voyages. Chau Nuong stood on the shore while the goods were loaded. Long after Canh Sinh had bid her farewell and boarded the ship, she stood on the beach straining for one last glimpse of his sails. Now that he was gone, she could weep freely. The tears she had suppressed so long ran down her cheeks—tears of pearl, not of water. Canh Sinh must

never see; Canh Sinh must never know. But now she was alone, and there was nothing to fear.

Day after day she went down to the shore to watch for Canh Sinh's return. Day after day she wept for him, till the beach was covered with pearls.

Then one morning far out on the horizon she saw his sails approaching. She watched them grow till the boat itself came into view. She searched the faces of the men on deck, seeking Canh Sinh's, but in vain. Fear gripped her heart; she ran toward the water to meet the ship.

Four of the crew bent down to pick up a stretcher. They stepped from the boat and walked up the beach toward the house.

Chau Nuong rushed after them. White and feverish, his lips parched and dry, Canh Sinh lay lifeless except for the shallow rise and fall of his chest.

One of the men answered her questions. "He fell sick on the voyage. We had to bring him home."

Her hands shaking, Chau Nuong ground herbs to powder, then stirred them into a cup of tea. She placed the cup on a tray and hurried to the sickroom.

Canh Sinh was lying in bed. A pearl-tear slipped from between her eyelids at the sight. She knelt by his side, calling his name softly. But he gave no response. His ashen lips parted now and then as he exhaled, but he showed no other sign of life.

Chau Nuong slipped her hand under his head. She pressed the cup to his lips and poured a little tea between them. She heard him swallow. Slowly, a few drops at a time, she fed him the medicine until the cup was empty. Then she rearranged the pillows and gently lowered his head. She pressed her hands to her face, trying to keep back the tears; but the pearls slipped through her fingers and covered the pillow where he lay.

For days she nursed him. Morning, noon, and evening she fed him rice gruel, patiently waiting while he swallowed. She cooked the rice and ground the medicine herself, unwilling to entrust his care to anyone else. Each day she gathered her tears and hid them in a chest, afraid that the servants would see them and wonder.

Then one day as she sat beside him, spooning the rice gruel into his mouth, he opened his eyes and looked at her. Her joy was so great that she dared not speak.

He looked around him in confusion.

"Where am I?" he asked.

"They brought you home sick," she managed to whisper.

He glanced at the empty rice bowl in her hand and at the medicine on the table. "You've been nursing me." His eyes rested on her tenderly. "What a pity I was unconscious!"

She could hold her tears back no longer. As they fell from her eyes, she buried her face in his pillow. She felt his arms pulling her up. She pressed him close, trying to forget for a moment the gulf that would ever be between them.

"My darling," he cried, his voice choked with emotion. "You love me, you do love me!" He lifted her face and pressed it to his.

Something hard struck Canh Sinh's cheek. He raised his head and saw the pearls streaming down Chau Nuong's face. Gently he plucked one from the corner of her eye and gazed at it in wonder.

"Chau Nuong, are you crying pearls?"

"I'm a fish fairy, the maid of the daughter of the Dragon King of the Waters. Several months ago I broke one of her favorite hairpins. The princess was so angry that she ordered me to leave the sea for a year. That was the day I met you on the beach."

Canh Sinh held her tight. "Never go back! Stay here and be my wife."

"I can't. When the year is up, I must return. When she ordered me to leave, I thought a year was so long. How could I live on land a whole year? But now! If only she had banished me for ten years or twenty or even forever!"

"There must be a way," Canh Sinh insisted.

"I've cried ten thousand tears, and I would cry ten thousand more to find that way. The beach where I waited for you is covered with pearls. While you were sick I filled three chests with my tears. But all in vain." She pushed one of the chests over to the bed and raised the cover for him to see.

Canh Sinh lifted a handful of pearls and pressed them to his lips. "Ah, Chau Nuong! I long to make you so happy you'd forget how to cry these lovely tears. As soon as I'm well, we'll go to the pagoda and pray for Quan Am's blessing. Perhaps she will help us."

Chau Nuong shook her head. "We can go if you wish, but it's useless. There's no way to change the celestial decrees."

Canh Sinh and Chau Nuong entered the pagoda. Each took incense and, bowing, placed the sticks in the urn before Quan Am, the goddess of mercy. When she had finished her prayer, Chau Nuong stood up.

Another girl stepped up to the incense. Chau Nuong gasped when she saw her. The two stood transfixed, staring at each other. They were perfect doubles.

"What's your name?" Chau Nuong blurted out.

"Van Chau," the girl replied, as much shaken as the other. "What's yours?"

Chau Nuong answered as if in a trance. "Where do you live?"

"On the Street of the Needleworkers. My father was an embroiderer. Our house is the one with the blue shutters."

The next afternoon while Canh Sinh was sleeping, Chau Nuong made her way to the Street of the Needleworkers. As soon as Van Chau saw her, she ran out to greet her.

The two chatted over tea and lotus-seed cakes.

"Do you embroider, too?" Chau Nuong asked, nodding toward the embroidery frame across the room. "May I look at your design?"

Van Chau led her over to the frame. "This is what I was working on when you came. Since my father's death, I've had to support my mother."

"You must work very hard."

"Yes," she admitted. "But it's honest work, and we have enough to eat."

"A girl with your talents must have many proposals of marriage."

Van Chau's face reddened. "I'm poor, and I have an aged mother to support. Not many men are interested under those circumstances."

"Those things wouldn't matter to a rich man."

"I suppose not, but when a rich man wants a poor girl, it's usually only for play."

"Not my cousin. He's a man of honor."

Van Chau smiled sadly. "It's hard for a poor girl to believe such a man exists."

"Then you must come and see for yourself," Chau Nuong invited. "Will you and your mother come for dinner tomorrow?"

A pang shot through Chau Nuong's heart when Van Chau and her mother arrived the next afternoon. But she ignored the hurt. There was no way she could change her own destiny, but at least she could ensure Canh Sinh's happiness.

Canh Sinh came into the room. Chau Nuong introduced him.

"This is the girl I met at the pagoda. Every time I look at her, I feel as if I were looking into a mirror."

Canh Sinh smiled. "I'd swear the two of you were made from the same mold." He studied first one, then the other in bewilderment. "If you exchanged clothes, I doubt whether your own mothers could tell you apart."

Van Chau's face reddened, and she lowered her eyes under Canh Sinh's gaze.

That evening Chau Nuong walked alone in the moonlight. In a few more weeks her stay on land would be over, and she would return to the sea. No, she mustn't cry. Better to think of Canh Sinh. She was sure that Van Chau loved him. And in time he, too, would learn to love her.

Chau Nuong heard footsteps behind her. Canh Sinh was running toward her.

"I thought you had gone," he panted. He clasped her hands, his eyes searching hers. "Why did you ask Van Chau to visit?"

"I hoped you wouldn't mind if I ask her to be my companion. She can keep me company when you're gone on your voyages. And I thought she could comfort you when I return to the Palace of the Waters."

"Comfort me?" He echoed her words, consternation mixed with the hurt in his voice. "Chau Nuong, did you think she could take your place? Because she looks like you? Do you think my love is so shallow, that I love you only for your beauty? I love you completely, to the depths of your soul. No one can ever take your place."

"Canh Sinh, I'm sorry." She hung her head as the tears rolled down her cheeks.

He put his hand under her chin and raised her face to his. "Don't cry, dear," he said, brushing the pearls from her eyes. "Van Chau is welcome to come if that makes you happy. But there will never be anyone for me but you."

In the weeks that followed, the three were often together. Chau Nuong tried to remain in the background, but Canh Sinh always made sure to include her. She purposely hung behind on their garden strolls, but Canh Sinh stayed with her instead of going ahead with Van Chau. Chau Nuong taught Van Chau all of Canh Sinh's likes and dislikes and all the little ways to please him, but he never seemed to notice. When he held out his cup for Van Chau to fill, his eyes were on Chau Nuong.

As the day of her departure drew near, Chau Nuong noticed all these things but told herself that time would work it out.

Late one afternoon she found Van Chau sitting alone in front of her embroidery frame. Chau Nuong watched her draw the gold thread through the cloth, filling in the mandarin ducks: symbols of wedded happiness.

"It's beautiful," she said. "It would make a lovely quilt for a newly married couple."

"All my life I've been making such things for others." A tear slipped from Van Chau's eye, dampening her work. "I don't know when I'll make one for myself."

"Isn't this one for you?"

"I thought it would be when I started it. But with each stitch I add to the embroidered ducks, the real ducks grow farther apart." She sighed.

"Van Chau, don't be discouraged. In time he will love you."

"It's you he loves, not me. Can't you see it? Why did you bring me here?"

Chau Nuong turned her head to hide her tears, but it was too late. Van Chau had seen.

Van Chau stared at her in amazement. She turned the gem around in her fingers, unable to believe her eyes.

"Yes, it's a pearl. I'm a sea fairy." Chau Nuong told her the story of her banishment. "Tonight the year is up, and I must return to the Palace of the Waters."

Van Chau took her hand. "Sister, you do love him, and he loves you. Your destiny is crueler than mine."

"Stay with him and comfort him when I'm gone. Someday he'll return your love."

"I will, for your sake. But I'm afraid he will never love me."

"He will, little sister. I know he will. I'm going to give you something to help you." She stood up. "Come to my room."

Chau Nuong opened a chest and drew out a long band of white silk. Standing in front of the mirror, she draped it over her back and shoulders, letting the ends float free at the sides.

She turned to Van Chau. "This is my fairy sash. I'm going to give it to you." She folded it and placed it in her hands. "If before the year is over, he's forgotten me and loves you, hide this sash away as a souvenir of our friendship. But if a year from today he still shows no sign of loving you, go to him that evening in the garden wearing this sash. May its magic power bring you his love! Now I must go. The time is growing short."

The two girls embraced tearfully. Van Chau stood in the doorway and watched as Chau Nuong walked away through the garden.

Canh Sinh was waiting for her beside the lotus pond. He took her hands in his as she approached.

"Darling, I've come to say good-bye."

"Will you come back?"

She shook her head. "No, I can never come back."

"Then I will follow you to the depths of the ocean."

She sighed. "Wait for me a year. I'll beg the Princess of the Waters to let me go. If she releases me, I'll meet you here in the garden a year from tonight. Wait for me in this very spot."

"Chau Nuong, you'll come! A year from tonight you'll come."

"I hope I can come." She blinked back the tears. "Now I must go. I mustn't be late."

She ran down the path toward the beach. As she reached the water's edge, she stepped down fearlessly. In the moonlight Canh Sinh saw her disappear into the waves, her long white sash billowing behind her. Far into the night, he sat on the shore, remembering her last words and the promised rendezvous a year away.

The next year dragged by like a river's current. Day by day Canh Sinh relived his memories of Chau Nuong, turning each one over and over in his mind as his fingers stroked the pearls she had left behind. Van Chau sought to comfort him; but he did not want to be comforted. Always Van Chau was there, but she was like a shadow on the edge of his consciousness, and he scarcely looked at her.

Finally the night of the tryst arrived. It was barely twilight when Canh Sinh came to the lotus pond. He stood on the bridge where he had held her hand that final night the year before. His heart ached with anticipation. He watched the sun go down, a crimson ball in the west. The moon was rising, a golden disk streaming light into the garden. Still she had not come. Fear crept into his heart. What if he should stand like this forever, alone and waiting? What if she should never return?

Then he saw the white sash. The breeze wafted it through the trees ahead of her as she came toward him in the moonlight. With a cry of joy he ran to meet her and clasped her in his arms. She returned his kiss, all the love pent up in her heart pouring forth in one great torrent.

"Chau Nuong," he cried, gazing deep into her eyes in the moon-light. "You've come back at last. How I've longed for this day. I've lived it a thousand times in my dreams!"

A tear glistened in her eye and rolled down her cheek. Now she knew there was no hope of his love. All her dreams lay as limp as the sash about her shoulders.

Canh Sinh touched her wet cheek in dismay. "Your tears!" he cried. "Where are the pearls?" He released her as the truth dawned on him. "You aren't Chau Nuong. You're Van Chau! Chau Nuong, where are you?"

In a frenzy he ran down the path toward the beach, calling her name. He dashed across the sand toward the water, plunging head-first into the sea. Far out in the ocean Van Chau saw a white sash rise above the waves. Two forms rose above the surface, locked in each other's arms, then disappeared beneath the foam.

Van Chau stood alone beside the sea. Not a ripple disturbed its face. She looked down and saw Canh Sinh's slippers where he had dropped them on the sand. Bending down, she picked them up and pressed them to her lips.

THIRD DAUGHTER

hird Daughter lifted the kettle from the fire. She aimed the spout downward, watching the water turn to amber as it filled the teapot. Carefully she replaced the cover and picked up the tray to carry it to the parlor.

The bead curtain parted; her mother stepped into the room. "I declare, girl, what makes you so slow?" Mrs. Luu demanded. "It's bad enough to have a face like a toad's. Do you have to have feet like a snail's as well?"

Third Daughter blinked back tears. "I'm sorry, Mother. I am coming."

"Well, I should hope so," Mrs. Luu huffed. "The guests are waiting. What will the young men think?"

Third Daughter kept her gaze on the floor as she followed her mother into the parlor. She'd hurry and fill the teacups as fast as she could and then get back to the kitchen, where she belonged—where she wouldn't have to see how beautiful First Daughter and Second Daughter looked in their silk and brocade dresses, their hair combed into high coiffures and gleaming with jeweled hairpins. They were as delicate as the china in front of them, as sparkling as crystal. But she, with her pimply complexion and straggly hair—all she could do with it was tie it with a ribbon and let it hang down her back—she was more like an earthenware pot. Useful, but certainly not pleasant to look at. In her plain black pants and simple white blouse, she looked more like a maid of the house than a daughter. Her mother was probably right, though. It would be a shame to waste expensive material on the likes of her. "Like putting peacock feathers on a crow," Mrs. Luu had once remarked. She glanced at her sisters across the table. It was true, as her mother often said: next to them she was like a catfish in a goldfish pond. No wonder they had attracted the attention of two such rich and handsome young men. Like Van Luong, whose cup she was filling now.

She leaned over to set the cup down in front of him. Suddenly it tipped over, filling his lap with amber liquid. With a gasp she dived after it. The teapot slipped from her hand and crashed to the floor, shattering into a thousand pieces on the tiling.

"You clumsy good-for-nothing girl!" her mother screeched. "Get out to the kitchen until I have time to deal with you."

Third Daughter fled from the room and sank down next to one of the water jars. Burying her face in her hands, she burst into tears. It was all her fault. She should have been tending to what she was doing, instead of feeling sorry for herself. She always ended up doing something stupid when she let herself think like that. The same thing had happened last week, and she had let the rice burn. Her mother had beat her and sent her to bed with no supper. But later her father had brought her a tray of food and rubbed ointment into the welts on her back. He didn't seem to mind how ugly she was; he loved her in spite of it. And he spoke up for her with her mother. Not that it did much good. Mrs. Luu always did exactly what she pleased, anyway.

"What are you doing behind that water jar?" Her mother was standing over her, glaring. "Just because no one would want your toad face, do you have to spoil your sisters' chances?" She reached for the long-handled feather duster that the maids used to clean cobwebs from the ceiling. "I won't dare to ask for as many bride gifts as I'd been intending to after that ridiculous scene." Third Daughter hid her face as the handle came down on her shoulder. "It's just lucky they don't know you're my daughter." The handle descended a second and a third time. "I told them you were a girl we'd just hired from the country."

"But, Mother!" Third Daughter started up, dodging the blows as best she could. "What will they say when they learn the truth? Let me go out and apologize."

"Apologize!" Mrs. Luu threw down the duster with a grunt and stepped to the cupboard. "I told them I was sending you back at once. So you'll have to go, of course." She wadded a handful of cold rice into a crude ball and laid it on a banana leaf, then topped it with a piece of dried fish, and rolled it all into an untidy bundle. "Here," she said, slapping it down on the counter. "At least you can't say I sent you away empty-handed." She turned toward the bead curtain, then stopped and looked back once more. "Now pack up your things and get out at once. And don't go crying to your father, or it'll be the worse for you."

Tears streaming down her face, Third Daughter wrapped her few garments in a bundle and stuffed the lunch into her pocket. Then she slipped out the back door and started down the road. She trudged wearily along, with no idea where she was going. The road led at last to a forest; she walked on, numb in body and spirit, with no plan but to set one foot before the other. At last her hunger made her remember the lunch in her pocket, and she sat down under a tree to eat.

A rustle of leaves behind her brought her to her feet. She stared at the old man who stood leaning on his staff, his long white beard reaching to his waist.

"I see you're eating lunch, child," his voice quavered. "Could you spare a little for a hungry old man?"

"Why, of course, sir." Third Daughter pinched the ball of rice into two equal portions and handed one to him.

"Thank you, child." He took the piece of fish that she held out to him. "You are very generous. But tell me, how do you come to be alone in the forest?"

"It's all because I'm so hopelessly ugly and clumsy." Third Daughter sobbed out the story to his sympathetic ears. "And now I don't know where I shall go or how I shall support myself."

"You don't look ugly to me, and I don't believe you're as clumsy as you say," the old man comforted her. "In fact, I believe your good fortune may just be beginning. I hear the king's palace is looking for someone to work in the kitchen. Why don't you apply for the job? But you'll be hot and dusty and your clothes will be soiled before you finish your journey. Stop and bathe at the spring you will find along this road as you near the other side of the forest."

She started to thank him, but the man had tapped on the ground three times with his staff and vanished as suddenly as he had appeared. "He must have been the Forest Spirit," she mused to herself as she hurried down the path he had indicated.

It was midafternoon when Third Daughter neared the edge of the forest. Just off the path a stream rushed down the side of a cliff. Hot and thirsty, Third Daughter laid her bundle beneath a tree and cupped her hands to take a drink. Then she stepped under the stream, letting the water wash over her, soaking her patched blouse and frayed pants. But what was happening? Where were the simple clothes she had been wearing? Long flowing sleeves now covered her arms, and her bodice was of a rich pink brocade.

Third Daughter ran off down the path, forgetting her bundle. The

road stretched before her; in the distance she could see the walls of the city and the roof of the king's palace.

The guards stepped aside as she approached the palace. "I hope I'm not too late," she began, but the guards interrupted her.

"Have no fear, miss; you are in good time," one of them said. "Come with us. We will take you to His Highness."

Third Daughter followed the guard to a pavilion within the palace walls. The room was filled with beautiful girls, each one lovelier than the last. Third Daughter drew back uneasily. No, just let her find the kitchen. She would be safe among the pots and pans. But if they wanted her to be a serving girl amidst all this splendor, she would never be able to do it.

She heard a voice boom above the hum of girlish chatter. "Isn't there anyone here that pleases you, son? Surely you can choose one from among the beauties of eighteen nations."

"Your Majesty, one more contestant has arrived." It was the guard standing next to her who was speaking.

She saw the king and the crown prince approaching her. What a handsome young man the prince was, far more handsome than her sisters' suitors. He was walking straight up to her. He must think she had come as one of the contestants. Surely he would cast her into prison for her presumption: that she, with her toad face, would dare to think herself good enough to marry the prince. But he looked kind. Perhaps if she explained. . . .

"Please, Your Highness, forgive me," she stammered. "The Forest Spirit sent me—"

The prince had taken her hand, drawing her to his side. "The Forest Spirit sent you!" he exclaimed. He turned to his father. "She must be a fairy. Only that would explain her beauty. Father, I have made my choice. She shall be my wife. And we shall build a shrine to express our thanks to the Forest Spirit for his benevolence."

Third Daughter's mind was spinning as she tried to understand what had happened. She knew the prince was right: it had been the Forest Spirit's benevolence that had caused it all. In her wildest dreams she had never imagined such splendor as she now saw on all sides of her. How happy her parents would be when they received the news.

"We will celebrate the wedding at once," she heard the king saying. "Call the queen; call all my mandarins; call the royal musicians!"

"Please, Your Majesty," Third Daughter interrupted him. "I must let my parents know. They must be here to share my happiness."

"We will send the royal palanquin to bring them to the palace." He turned to an attendant to give the order.

As soon as the man stepped from the room, a rumbling shook the palace. The Thunder Spirit, his drum on his back, was winging his way toward Mrs. Luu, his lightning ax ready to strike the cruel woman.

Rain was pelting the palace roof. The King beamed at his son and Third Daughter. "Not only the Forest Spirit," he said, "but Heaven itself is showering us with its blessings."

$\mathcal{S}$ECOND-IN-$\mathcal{C}$OMMAND

$\mathcal{H}$oa Moc Lan drew the bowstring back till her fingers touched her cheek, then let the arrow fly. She watched it speed through the air and strike the target dead center. A perfect bull's-eye—again.

Mr. Hoa grinned as he pulled himself to his feet. "That was beautiful, daughter," he said, patting her shoulder. "I couldn't be more proud if it were your brother. Not that Minh Long isn't passable with a bow. But he doesn't have your talent for it. Or for the sword or the lance either, for that matter."

Moc Lan squeezed her father's hand. "It's all thanks to you, Father. You've taught me everything I know."

He chuckled softly to himself, pleased to be reminded of it. "Time was when I could beat you, too. But not anymore. If we took a turn with our swords today, you'd win easily."

"Father, you've been ill this winter." She stroked his wan cheek. "But you'll soon be your old self again now that spring is here."

A noise outside the gate made Moc Lan glance up. She frowned when she saw the hat over the top of the wall. It looked as if it belonged to one of the king's messengers.

"Stay here, Father," she said, handing her bow to him. "I'll see who it is." She ran down the path toward the gate.

"King's orders for Mr. Hoa," the messenger announced as Moc Lan peered out. She took the roll of paper from his hand. "He's to report immediately for military duty."

Moc Lan closed the gate and sank back against it. She had heard rumors about bandit rebels who were raiding the countryside along the border. She unrolled the message and skimmed the characters written on it. Naturally the king would want her father. He had proved himself a brave and skillful warrior many times in the past. But now he was old, and he had not been well for the past several months.

Moc Lan carried the message inside and handed it to him. "You can't go, Father," she said. "Let me take your place."

Minh Long stepped to his father's side, reading the message over his shoulder. "I'll go," he said quietly. "It's my duty to go."

"You know I'm the better fighter." Moc Lan faced her brother, her eyes determined.

Mr. Hoa put up his hand for silence. "That's ridiculous. A girl can't join the army."

"I can wear your armor and Minh Long's clothes. No one will know I'm a girl." She stood facing the frowns of her father and brother. "From the time Minh Long and I were children you instructed us side by side. You said your daughter had the right to learn everything that your son was taught. Now that I'm grown, would you deny me the right to use my skills to help my family and my country? Would you make me stick to my loom and spend my days tending the silkworms? I will have time enough for that in the future. Father, with your permission, Minh Long and I will try our skills against each other. The winner will wear your armor into battle."

Mr. Hoa led the way out to the courtyard. Moc Lan and Minh

Long unsheathed their swords, and the duel began. The clang of metal filled the yard as the swords clashed again and again. Moc Lan lunged; Minh Long parried. Minh Long thrust at her; Moc Lan foiled the blow. Then with a twist of her wrist Moc Lan sent her brother's sword flying. She stepped back, her head high, her face flushed; and Minh Long, smiling, acknowledged defeat.

Mr. Hoa's eyes shone as he walked toward his daughter. "I've seen few men handle a sword as well," he declared. "You have earned the right to wear my armor. But as to whether it can make you look like a man," he added, his hand on her shoulder, "only time will tell. You're as beautiful as you are talented, and the excitement of conquest only makes you lovelier."

"Thank you, Father." Moc Lan felt the red in her cheeks deepen. "I promise to do everything in my power to bring glory to the name of Hoa—a glory that will last a thousand years."

The three returned to the house. Moc Lan changed into the tunic and baggy pants that Minh Long chose for her. She pulled the ornaments from her hair and untied the band that held the front looped into a roll on top of her head. A shimmering ebony mass hung far down her back. Moc Lan sighed as she looked into the mirror. She reached for the scissors and snipped her hair off just below her shoulders. She combed back what was left, rolled it into a compact knot on top of her head, and bound it with the narrow scarf her brother had given her. She stepped back, examined herself again in the mirror, and smiled with satisfaction. Even her father would have to admit that now she looked more like Minh Long than Moc Lan.

Her family was waiting for her when she went down the stairs. Her father smiled when he saw her. "I'm afraid I was wrong. You make a handsome young man indeed." He handed his armor to her piece by piece. "The house of Hoa will not be poorly represented in this campaign," he added as she placed the helmet on her head.

Moc Lan adjusted her sword in its sheath and turned to embrace her parents. She swallowed down the lump that rose in her throat. How long would it be before she saw her family again? But she must not think of that. She had a duty to them and to her country, and her first obligation was to fulfill it. Pulling herself to her full height, Moc Lan walked to her horse and sprang into the saddle. Then, taking the reins, she gave the animal a nudge and sped away.

Her cape billowed behind her like a banner as her horse galloped toward the soldiers' camp. She threw back her shoulders, inhaling the fragrance of new grass and the perfume of a thousand spring flowers. Birds sang in the treetops and butterflies flitted among the blossoms.

The sun stood straight overhead when she saw the highway in the distance. To the left, another fork joined the main road. She could make out a figure approaching: a horseman dressed in armor.

The young man raised his arm in greeting as they neared each other.

"Are you off to join the army, too?" he called. Moc Lan nodded. "Then let's travel together," he said. "It's a long road, alone; good company will make it shorter. My name is Ly Quang."

"I would welcome your company," Moc Lan responded. "My name is Hoa Minh Long."

"Minh Long," Ly Quang repeated. "Bright Dragon. A noble name. May it be a good omen for your future."

Moc Lan smiled, forcing herself to meet her companion's eyes boldly. Acting the part of a man was not as easy as she had thought, especially with someone as handsome as Ly Quang.

It was nearly evening by the time they reached the camp and presented themselves to the commander in chief. The recruits spent the next several days in testing and training as they were organized into units. The commander himself led one group, and he placed Moc Lan in charge of the left flank and Ly Quang the right.

The next morning they rode off to fight the rebels. The battle raged until evening, when the rebels, overwhelmed by their losses, fled toward the border. Moc Lan and Ly Quang led their men in pursuit. They won a brilliant victory, although the rebel captain managed to escape across the river with what was left of his forces.

Soldiers and officers alike celebrated the victory that night. Every tent rang with song and laughter. The commander joined Moc Lan and Ly Quang at their table. "I am promoting you for your performance today," he said to Moc Lan. "You are now second-in-command."

Moc Lan glanced at Ly Quang and saw her excitement mirrored in his eyes. She felt her cheeks redden.

"This calls for a celebration," Ly Quang exclaimed. He set out three drinking bowls and lifted the flask of wine to fill them. The first he presented to the commander. Then he took up the second and placed it in Moc Lan's hands.

Ly Quang's fingers brushed hers lightly as she took the bowl from him. Her heart raced so wildly that she wondered how Ly Quang himself could not hear it pounding. She steadied her hands against the bowl and raised it to her lips, staring into the wine.

The commander broke the silence. "The rebels are in retreat for the time being," he was saying. "But I know their leader. He won't give up. As soon as he's regrouped his men, he'll be back to attack us."

Moc Lan and her troops stood watching near the river. All was quiet; for the past several days there had been no sign of the enemy. Suddenly the startled caws of a thousand birds brought Moc Lan to attention. Across the river a great flock of crows rose into the air. They flew toward the bank and out over the water.

"Stay on guard," Moc Lan ordered the men around her. "There will be action soon."

She hurried to the commander's tent. "The rebels must be getting ready to attack," she warned him, telling him what she had seen. Together they planned their strategy for the battle.

It was well past midnight when the rebels stole across the river and crept into the camp. The king's men were ready for them. Although the rebels fought desperately, they were repulsed at every turn. At last,

just before dawn, the remaining rebel forces took to their heels and made for the river. Moc Lan led her soldiers after them.

"This time they mustn't escape," she urged the men as she leapt into the water. "After them! We must take their leader."

The chief spun around. He lunged at Moc Lan with his sword. Again she was ready, and she parried his stroke skillfully. They thrust at each other, seeking an advantage. But they were well matched; neither was able to break through the other's defense. Metal clanged against metal. The water turned cloudy, then muddy, from their struggle. All at once Moc Lan found an opening, and she drove her sword deep. The rebel chief's sword tore into her arm as he fell at her feet.

Ly Quang appeared at her side, panting for breath. "Let me help you," he offered. He took her hand, guiding her to the tent. "Let's get you out of that shirt so we can clean the wound."

Moc Lan shook her head. "No, just cut the sleeve, please. It's already too badly torn to be saved."

Ly Quang did as she asked. She winced with pain, but soon Ly Quang was applying a salve of soothing herbs and wrapping clean cloths around it.

Now the campaign was nearly finished, and the troops would be returning home. But the thought of seeing her family again turned bitter as Moc Lan realized that soon she and Ly Quang would be parting.

The flap of the tent lifted. The commander entered. "The rebel chief is in our custody, thanks to you," he announced, sitting down next to Moc Lan. "The rest of the bandits have surrendered. I'm leaving now to take them to the king and to tell him of your bravery. But I couldn't go without offering my congratulations in person."

"Thank you, sir." Moc Lan flushed with pleasure. "It has been a privilege to serve our king and country under your leadership."

"It has been a privilege on my part. I hope I shall have the further privilege of seeing our relationship become even closer. I have a daughter about your age and have yet to meet a man that I would rather have as my son-in-law."

Moc Lan drew a sharp breath. She studied the floor, struggling to frame a suitable reply. "Sir, I am deeply honored," she finally answered. Her voice was low and the words came haltingly. "But I dare not accept your offer without my parents' permission."

"Spoken like a dutiful son!" The commander rose to his feet, clapping Moc Lan's shoulder approvingly. "I shall give you a few days at home with your parents. Then I shall come and speak with them in person."

Moc Lan's heart sank as he turned and left the tent. What would become of her now? She dreaded the thought of his visit and what would happen when he learned the truth.

But Ly Quang was speaking. "What an honor has come to you, brother!" He clasped her hand, pressing it warmly. "I only wish that you had a sister so that I could ask for her hand as well."

Moc Lan's heart skipped a beat. Half of her wanted to laugh, the other half to burst into tears. "I'm going to lie down," she finally said. "I'm feeling weaker than I thought." She unrolled her mat and sank back against the pillow, then turned to the wall. As the tears rolled down her cheeks, she drew the blanket up over her face.

Moc Lan sat staring out of her window. One hand rested on the frame of her loom. The other lay idle in her lap, holding the shuttle. It had been three weeks since she and Ly Quang had clasped each other's arms at the crossroads and vowed to remain brothers for a thousand lifetimes. Then Ly Quang had ridden out of her life as quickly and as quietly as he had entered it, leaving nothing behind but her aching heart and the longing that filled her dreams. Destiny had brought them together. Now it would just as surely keep them apart.

Moc Lan heard a shout and looked down into the courtyard. The gate hung open. Her father and brother were welcoming a long train of arrivals. Moc Lan drew back from the window. The commander was speaking with her father. Behind them stood Ly Quang holding a lacquered box inlaid with mother-of-pearl. It could contain only one thing: gifts for a prospective bridegroom.

She turned at the sound of footsteps outside her room. Minh Long stood in the doorway. His lips were pulled into a straight line, but his eyes twinkled with laughter. "Father wants you to come down," he said.

Moc Lan descended the stairs and hesitantly entered the room. Her eyes dropped in embarrassment at the stares that greeted her.

"Here is your second-in-command," Mr. Hoa told them, "not Hoa Minh Long but Hoa Moc Lan, my daughter. She has excelled with the bow and the sword since her childhood, so when the summons came for me—you can see for yourselves how old and weak I have become—she insisted on going in my stead. I do have a son, Minh Long," he added, drawing him forward as well. "He, too, is skilled with the lance and the sword. But I had only one suit of armor. His sister challenged him and won the right to wear it."

The commander smiled as Mr. Hoa finished. "The house of Hoa has a right to be proud," he declared. "I came here today to offer the hand of my daughter to Hoa Minh Long. I see no reason"—he glanced from Mr. Hoa to his son— "to change my intention. I should count myself fortunate to join my own family with such an illustrious line." He took the box from Ly Quang and placed it in Mr. Hoa's hands. He turned back to Ly Quang with a smile. "As for your daughter, I think my companion would also like to speak a few words."

Ly Quang stepped forward. "Sir, I told your daughter once that if she had a sister I would ask for her hand. But fate has been even kinder to me. I would like to ask your permission to return day after tomorrow with betrothal gifts of my own."

Mr. Hoa turned to his daughter. "You have been this man's comrade," he said. "You have fought beside him in battle. Do you judge him worthy to be your husband, to be joined with you in the bonds of a hundred-year friendship?"

Moc Lan brushed her long sleeve over her eyes. "Yes, Father," she murmured. "That has been my dream since the day our paths joined at the highway—that the red ties of marriage might bind my feet to his forever, for a thousand lifetimes."

THE GOLDEN CARP

M̲inh Chi set his pack in front of the big iron gate, relieved to have it off his back. It held just a few clothes and some books. But even a small pack can become heavy when you carry it all day, for several days.

He looked down at his slippers, wincing at the rip made by the rock he had stumbled over that morning. This wasn't the way he had planned to arrive at his fiancée's house, tattered, soiled, and travel-worn. His father had been the richest man in the province when he had signed Minh Chi's marriage contract with the Tran family—rich enough to have organized the grandest of processions to escort his son to the bride's house on their wedding day: carts freshly painted in bright reds and yellows, horses draped with brocades and decked with flowers, and Minh Chi himself dressed in robes fit for a prince. But now his parents were dead, their riches gone. Minh Chi was alone in the world.

No, not really alone. Unlike most orphans, he would have no worries about a place to live or having enough to eat while he finished his studies. His future in-laws had always been like second parents to him. Minh Chi's father and Mr. Tran had been friends since childhood; as they grew older, they had promised each other that their children would someday marry. He smiled when he thought of Thanh Tung, his wife-to-be. How she must have grown in the two years since he had last seen her! He remembered how they had played together in the garden. He had to keep reminding himself that by now she was a young lady—as sweet and beautiful as she had always been, he was sure.

The gate opened a crack. The stern face of an old servant frowned at his mud-spattered pants.

"Who are you, and what do you want?" he demanded.

"I'm Luong Minh Chi, Mr. Tran's son-in-law."

The man's eyes swept over him once again before he opened the gate just enough for Minh Chi to squeeze through.

"All right, come on in," he muttered. "But you'll have to wait here till Mr. Tran comes." Without another word the servant turned and walked into the house, leaving Minh Chi standing in the garden. Strange that he hadn't taken him into the house and offered him a chair. Minh Chi sat down on a rock to wait.

An hour passed, and then another. Perhaps the servant had forgotten to tell his master of Minh Chi's arrival. He shifted his position wearily. How hungry he was! He had had nothing to eat since early that morning, and now the sun was sinking over the horizon.

Minh Chi stood up, raising his pack to his back, and started toward the house. As he neared the steps he caught sight of a blue robe among the trees. He stopped in surprise, as Mr. Tran turned around to face him.

"Father! How are you?" He bowed in greeting. An embarrassing silence followed. "Perhaps the servant forgot to let you know I'd come."

"No, I knew you were here." His voice sounded gruff. "I've been very busy today." He started toward the door. "Well, now that you're here, come on inside."

Minh Chi followed his father-in-law into the house. Mr. Tran motioned for him to sit down.

"I regretted to hear about your parents' unfortunate death," he began. "I'm sorry I was unable to attend the funeral."

"I understand, Father. It would have been a long way for you to go."

"I suppose you're still keeping up the house."

He shook his head sadly. "The funeral took everything that was left after I'd paid my father's debts. Didn't you receive my message?"

"Yes, of course. I was expecting you." He cleared his throat. "What are your plans for the future?"

"Naturally I intend to finish my studies and to compete in the next imperial exams."

"I'm sure you realize that we can make no definite plans for the wedding until you do."

Minh Chi was taken aback. "But the contract—"

Mr. Tran laughed. "That contract was signed a good many years ago, under very different circumstances."

Minh Chi rose to his feet in indignation. "When my parents were alive, you treated me like your own son; but now that I'm poor you want to break the marriage contract—"

"Now, now, my boy. Who said anything about breaking the contract? It's up to you to concentrate on your studies. We'll see how you do on the exams." He stood up. "I'll call Lao Ba and have him take you to your room and bring you something to eat."

The servant led him down long, dimly lit corridors to an annex. The doors creaked as he pulled them open. Inside, dust covered the rough wooden furniture; spiders' webs linked chair to chair and bench to bench. Minh Chi flicked the dust off one of the chairs with the back of his coat and sank down. Homesickness swept over him, and he was glad when Lao Ba left the room. He walked over to the bed and lay down, too tired even to undress. In a few seconds he was asleep.

The sunlight shining through his window awoke him the next morning. There was one advantage to his room: the lovely view of the garden. He opened the doors and stepped onto the veranda. A path led past a lotus pond, twisting and turning among rows of trees and flowers. An early morning walk would do him good, he decided; when his mind and body were refreshed, he would be able to study better.

Watching the butterflies flit among the trees and the songbirds hop from branch to branch, he relived his childhood visits to the garden. He wondered whether Thanh Tung knew that he had arrived.

Rounding a turn in the path, he saw her bending over a rosebush. How lovely she had become! He stood looking at her, reluctant to speak lest he break the spell.

Suddenly she raised her head and looked at him. He smiled in anticipation.

"Thanh Tung!" he cried. "I was just wishing I could see you."

A frown shaded her features. "It's not good for us to meet alone. Someone might see us."

"No one could blame us for exchanging a few words here in broad daylight." He smiled. "Remember those long walks we used to take in this garden? How I used to pick flowers and put them in your hair?"

"We aren't children any longer, Minh Chi. Things are different now."

"But we're betrothed to each other. Aren't you glad to see me?"

"It'll be years before we can get married. It's too early to think of flowers and moonlight. Better to concentrate on your lamp and books."

She edged away to look at another blossom. Minh Chi stood,

stunned by her words, his eyes stinging with tears. He turned and walked slowly up the path toward his room.

Something gold flitted on the surface of the water as he passed the lotus pond. He leaned against the railing and looked down. A golden carp was swimming in and out among the lily pads. Fascinated, he watched the fish dart through the water, then leap into the air, its scales sparkling in the sunlight.

"What a pleasant life!" He sighed. "It must be nice to be a fish." He watched it leap up again in a spray of water and then dive back into the pond. "I wonder if you're ever lonely, golden carp. I wonder if you can see me or hear what I'm saying." As if in answer to his question, the fish raised its head above the water and somersaulted into the air. "You're my only friend in this cold, unfriendly place. You're the only one who seems glad to see me."

With a sigh he walked into the house and took out his books to study.

Summer turned to fall and fall to winter, with Minh Chi still an involuntary recluse. Three times a day his meals were brought to him. Lao Ba was the only person he ever saw; Thanh Tung and her parents avoided him, and he was never included in any of the family activities. From early morning till late at night he pored over his books, determined to succeed. But often, in his loneliness, discouragement got the better of him and he left his books to seek comfort in the garden. The lotus pond was his favorite spot. He loved to watch the golden carp leap in the water and dive for the chunks of rice he threw to it. In his craving for companionship he talked to the fish and told it his troubles. Sometimes he could almost imagine that it heard and understood him and knew that he, too, had nowhere else to go.

As the days grew colder, he went outdoors less often. He stood by his window, shivering with cold. He had no warm clothes, and his requests for firewood were ignored. He thought of the fish in the pond and wondered idly if it were as cold as he.

All alone at the bottom of the pond lay the golden carp. It had been days since Minh Chi had come out to stand on the bridge and talk to her. How could he know that she missed him—that under her scales beat the heart of a fairy who had come to love him? Kim Nuong sighed. If only she were Thanh Tung, he would never be sad or lonely again. She would bring him wood and build a fire for him with her own hands. She would weave a coat for him and pad it well to keep out the winter winds. They would walk in the garden under the moon and stand on the bridge together—and watch the golden carp in the water.

How dull her life was, though she'd never thought of it before—swimming, all day swimming around this narrow pond. Suddenly the society of the big green turtle and her sister fish was no longer attractive. People said the world was full of sorrow and disappointment, but it would be worth it to be loved by someone like Minh Chi. If only she were Thanh Tung!

A wild idea flitted through her mind. She could assume human form at any time. Why not Thanh Tung's? Minh Chi loved Thanh Tung. What if he thought she was Thanh Tung?

Kim Nuong swam to the edge of the pond and leapt up onto the path. As soon as her fins struck the ground, she was transformed into a beautiful girl. She wondered what Minh Chi was doing now. It was so late, perhaps he was already in bed. She would just creep to the window and peek in.

Poor boy! He had fallen asleep over his books, his head propped up on one arm. She pushed against the door. It opened easily. She

tiptoed over to the table. His head was only inches from the lamp. Reaching across, she moved it away from him.

Wide awake now, he stared at her in astonishment. "Thanh Tung!" he exclaimed. "Is it really you, or am I dreaming?"

She smiled. "It's really me, dear."

"You've finally come! Why have you been avoiding me all these months?"

"Please try to understand. My parents have forbidden me to see you, and I didn't dare disobey them. I know how hard it's been for you and how badly they've treated you. If you only knew how miserable I've been, knowing that you were in the same house and not being able to meet you. Finally I couldn't stand it any longer; I had to see you." A tear slid from between her eyelids and rolled down her cheek.

"Don't cry, dear." He reached up and brushed it away. "It's enough to know that you still love me."

"I mustn't stay long." She started to leave. "My father would punish me if he found me here."

He walked her to the door, holding her hand to detain her.

"Thanh Tung, when can I see you again? Where can we meet?"

"I'll come tomorrow evening," she promised him. "I'll wait for you outside your window."

She slipped out, ran down the path, and hid behind a tree until he had gone back inside. Then she stepped into the pond, shrinking into a fish as soon as she touched the water.

The winter passed quickly now. Minh Chi studied hard all day, scarcely noticing the cold as he anticipated the evening walks with his sweetheart. Spring came, bringing warm days; but Minh Chi and Kim Nuong were hardly aware of the difference, for the glow in their hearts was the same. The rest of the family were in the midst of New Year festivities; but the lovers, wrapped up in themselves, took little notice of the holiday season.

They stood one evening on the bridge overlooking the pond.

"Do you know, Thanh Tung," he told her, "there's the prettiest golden carp in this pond. I used to like to watch it flit among the water lilies and leap into the air. Whenever I was sad, I'd come down here and talk to it." He continued whimsically. "I really think it must know all about us by now."

She laughed. "No doubt it does."

"Maybe I should ask it when your father will let us get married."

He took her hand. "I try so hard to study so I can succeed in the exams. But even if I do, I'm not sure your father will keep his promise."

"Don't worry, dear. Even if he doesn't, I will."

He put his arm around her. "You will what, darling?"

"I'll follow you," she whispered, "wherever you go."

He clasped her in his arms. "I'll study hard to be worthy of you."

"It's late now. I'd better go in." Kim Nuong drew his head down and kissed him, then turned and ran off through the trees.

He stood for some minutes after she had gone, dazed by what she had just said. There was so much he wanted to tell her—words that had often been on the tip of his tongue, but which he had never dared to speak. Suddenly he wanted to pour out his whole heart to her and let her know how much he loved her. He didn't dare to go to her room, but maybe he could catch her before she got there.

He followed the path around the other side of the house to the wing where she slept. How well he remembered this part of the garden! He hid behind a tree, watching for her. Someone was coming toward him. His heart beat fast. It was Thanh Tung.

He ran to her, clasping her hands in his.

"Darling," he cried, "I couldn't wait till tomorrow to tell you how much I love you!"

She pulled her hands away, leaping back from him. "How dare you come here?" she demanded. "How dare you touch me like that?"

He was stunned. "It's me, Minh Chi. I didn't mean to scare you. I only came back to tell you—"

"I don't know what you're talking about. Go away now, and don't ever come here again."

She ran toward the house, leaving him alone and crushed. Slowly, with head bowed, he walked back to his room. As he passed the lotus pond, he noticed Lao Ba and several other servants standing outside his door. As he came nearer, they grabbed his arms.

"Come with us," Lao Ba ordered. "Mr. Tran wants to see you."

They half pushed, half dragged him to the front of the house and into the living room, where the Tran family was waiting for him. Mr. Tran rose and strode toward him.

"So that's the way you repay my hospitality," he shouted in his face, "by molesting my daughter."

"Father!" Minh Chi stammered, too shocked to reply.

"Don't ever call me 'Father' again. What do you mean by going to my daughter's room, lying in wait for her, then jumping out and embracing her?"

"Sir, Thanh Tung came to me first, or I wouldn't have dared." He turned to her, sitting on the divan, a look of injured dignity on her face. "Please tell him, Thanh Tung," he pleaded. "Tell him what you told me this evening, or else give me permission to speak."

"Of all the impudence!" She rolled her eyes. "Father, why do we have to listen to his lies? Don't we have enough grounds to break the marriage contract?"

"Break the marriage contract! Half an hour ago you promised to follow me wherever I went, and now you want to break the marriage contract!"

"I'd rather die than marry him," she cried, ignoring Minh Chi's words. "If you don't dissolve the contract, I'll kill myself."

Mr. Tran turned toward his daughter. "I'll take care of everything," he promised. "We'll have our lawyer come tomorrow morning."

"I want to do it tonight." Thanh Tung stamped her foot. "Force him to sign it," she shouted, waving her hand in Minh Chi's direction. "Throw him into jail if he won't."

"Thanh Tung, everything will be taken care of. You can be sure

I wouldn't let you marry such a good-for-nothing." He turned to Minh Chi. "Go back to your room. I'll talk to you tomorrow."

Hurt, indignation, and shame welling up in his breast, Minh Chi went back to his room. Hurriedly he collected his books and clothes and stuffed them into his bag. Let them do what they wanted about the marriage contract. Let them tear it into a thousand bits and cast it to the four winds, he didn't care. He would not sleep another night in their house. He winced with the memory of each indignity he had suffered there. As long as there was hope of Thanh Tung's love, he could bear it. But now he knew her for the two-faced creature she was.

He pushed the door open and strode down the path, past the lotus pond, as fast as he could, anxious to distance himself from the place where he had been treated so shamefully. He heard footsteps behind him. He quickened his pace, determined that they would not overtake him and bring him back.

He reached the wall, threw his pack over, then climbed after it. Jumping down on the other side, he started for town.

"Minh Chi!" He heard someone call his name. "Wait for me."

Anger welled up in his breast at the sound of Thanh Tung's voice. He turned and faced her.

"Why are you following me?" he demanded. "Why don't you go back to your father? You told him you'd rather be dead than marry me."

"Please, don't you understand?" Kim Nuong put her hand on his arm.

"Don't touch me! That's what you said to me tonight." He pushed her away. "What are you trying to do? Hold me here till your father comes? Don't waste your time. Tear up the contract. Marry whomever you like. I'll never come back again."

"Minh Chi, please believe me. What I told you in the garden tonight is true. Don't blame me for what I said at the house. My father made me do it. He threatened to kill me if I didn't." Tears rolled down her cheeks. "What could I do? I thought you would know me well enough to understand."

"You could have given me some sign."

"I didn't dare. I knew he would never allow our marriage, so the only thing I could do was to make you so angry that you would leave, and then I could follow you. Now we're free. We'll never go back to that house again."

"Thanh Tung, are you sure? I couldn't bear to be hurt again."

"I'll never hurt you again. I promise."

He put his arm around her, and they walked on together.

They made their way down the narrow streets, keeping in the shadows. Suddenly they heard the beat of a drum in the distance.

Minh Chi gripped Kim Nuong's hand in excitement. "It's the unicorn dancers. I'd almost forgotten this was New Year's week."

The street swarmed with people, young and old, come to watch the parade. Acrobats leapt in the air and the musicians beat on their drums, leading the way for the unicorn, an awe-inspiring creature whose many-colored mask and garments hid from view the bodies of the men who swayed to and fro beneath them. The lanterns hanging from the houses had all been lighted, and good-luck money wrapped in red paper hung from every window, waiting for the unicorn to climb up and claim it.

Suddenly Kim Nuong caught sight of a familiar face across the road. Lao Ba was staring at them as if unable to believe his eyes. Kim Nuong clutched at Minh Chi's sleeve, whispering to him what she had seen.

Together they jostled their way through the crowd to the open road. As they rounded a corner, men blocked the path ahead, surrounding them.

Lao Ba stepped forward and pointed a finger at Kim Nuong. "There! I told you I'd seen that good-for-nothing making off with the young mistress. Though I wouldn't have believed it of her, if I hadn't seen it myself."

"One never knows what to believe of young people nowadays," one of the others remarked, and the rest guffawed. "Come along, you two lovers, unless you can give us a reason to keep our mouths shut. I'm sure the master will reward our efforts."

Grasping him by the collar, the servants dragged Minh Chi back to the house and thrust him in front of Mr. Tran.

"We found this scoundrel eloping with the young miss."

Mr. Tran glared past Minh Chi at the servants. "Nonsense! My daughter's upstairs in bed. She wouldn't have anything to do with that worthless fellow." He strode to the stairway. "Thanh Tung, come down here immediately."

Thanh Tung appeared on the stairs. Minh Chi gaped at her as she walked down the steps into the room.

"You see my daughter," Mr. Tran shouted, taking her hand and leading her forward. "Now, what's all this foolishness about?"

"Then who's this?" Lao Ba shoved Kim Nuong forward.

The girls stood face to face, staring at each other, while everyone looked first at one, then at the other, unable to believe their eyes. The two were as alike as if they had been cut with the same die.

"Which one of you is Thanh Tung?" her father demanded.

"I am," the two chorused as one.

Hands on hips, Thanh Tung glared at her double. "How dare you come into my house, impersonating me?"

Kim Nuong took a step forward. "How dare you sneak into my room and sleep in my bed?"

"You must be some kind of evil spirit." Thanh Tung scowled at her, then turned to her father. "Can't you get rid of this creature? Can't you see she's an impostor?"

Kim Nuong looked at Mr. Tran, a hurt expression in her eyes. "Father, are you going to let that witch call me names? Don't you know your own daughter?"

Mr. Tran gazed from one to the other, shaking his head. "I don't know what to do," he moaned. "Let me call your mother."

As soon as Mrs. Tran entered the room, both girls ran to embrace her. The woman stepped back in bewilderment and collapsed into a chair as the girls knelt at her side, each pleading her case.

"There's only one thing to do," Mr. Tran declared. "We'll send for Judge Bao Cong. He'll be able to tell us which of you is a spirit and which is our daughter. For tonight, both of you can go upstairs and try to get along."

The girls glared at each other as they turned toward the stairs.

As soon as Thanh Tung was asleep, Kim Nuong crept out of the house to the pond. She swam around until she found the big green turtle.

"Bao Cong will know I'm a carp fairy," she told him, "and he'll expose me. But if you impersonate Bao Cong, no one will be able to prove which of you is the true judge and which is the false."

The turtle laughed. "It's a wonderful plan," he said. "You can depend on me. All the other fish will help, too."

Early the next morning Bao Cong arrived, followed by his entourage. They had hardly gotten through the gate when another group entered, each man the image of his counterpart in the first group.

The judges sat down side by side, each ignoring his double, as if he himself were the only one of importance present. Mr. Tran stared helplessly from one to the other.

Thanh Tung and Kim Nuong came before the judges.

Bao Cong pointed his finger at Kim Nuong. "This one is a spirit," he declared without hesitation. "The other girl is Tran Thanh Tung."

"Sir, I beg to differ with you," the turtle spirit countered. "It's obvious to me that this girl is the true one"—he pointed to Kim Nuong—"and the other is a spirit."

Bao Cong faced his adversary, indignant. "Being a spirit yourself, how could one expect an honest judgment from you?"

"My high position restrains me from answering you in kind," the turtle spirit replied calmly, "much as I resent your impersonating me."

"Both of you must be punished," Bao Cong insisted, glaring from the turtle spirit to Kim Nuong. "You have no right to be here, masquerading as mortals, meddling in the affairs of humans."

The turtle spirit raised his hand for silence. "Now, friend, let's listen to reason. We could sit here forever accusing each other, accomplishing nothing. We're here to judge a case. Here are two girls, alike in every detail. The parents, even the mother who bore her and cared for her so intimately, are incapable of distinguishing which one is their daughter and which one is the impostor. Who then can tell?

"This girl is betrothed to the young man you see standing over there. They were childhood sweethearts. Who could distinguish the false from the true better than he? No one can deceive the heart of love. Let's call Minh Chi and ask him to tell us who the real Thanh Tung is."

Minh Chi stepped toward the girls. Thanh Tung sniffed and turned away, her nose in the air. Kim Nuong gazed at him tenderly, her eyes glistening with tears. Minh Chi took her hand in his.

"This is the real Thanh Tung," he declared. "As you said, sir, we've loved each other since we were children. When I was wealthy, her parents were proud to call me son; now that I'm poor, they've conspired to separate us. But she hasn't changed. I have no idea who this other girl is," he added, pointing to Thanh Tung, "but I believe she may be an evil spirit her parents conjured up to separate us."

Bao Cong sprang to his feet, his face red with indignation. "That's absurd," he cried.

The turtle spirit laid a hand on his arm. "Friend, the solution is easy," he said. "There are two girls here. One who loves the young man and one doesn't. Let the one who loves Minh Chi go with him. The other girl may stay with the parents. Does everyone agree?"

Thanh Tung glowered at Kim Nuong. "No! She's an impostor. I demand that she be punished."

"Will you marry Minh Chi, then?" the turtle spirit asked, turning to her. "According to the contract, Minh Chi must have a wife."

Thanh Tung stood scowling from one to the other. At last she stamped her foot. "Let him have her, then. Only get them both out of my sight."

Minh Chi stood with his arm around Kim Nuong.

"Wait a minute," Bao Cong interrupted. He turned to Minh Chi. "Young man, are you willing to take the risk of marrying a fairy?"

Minh Chi faced him resolutely. "Sir, whoever or whatever she is, I will always love her."

The turtle spirit smiled at the pair before him. "Go, then," he said, "with our blessing."

Minh Chi took Kim Nuong's hand, and together the two turned to leave. Outside the gate he stopped to kiss her.

"I'm so glad I found out the truth," he told her. "Why did you let me think that you were the one who had treated me so badly?"

She smiled up at him. "It's a long story, dear, and a strange one—about a golden carp and a poor student. Someday I'll tell it all to you, but you may not believe it even when I do."

回　　回　　回

$\mathcal{A}$UTHOR'S $\mathcal{N}$OTES

A FRIEND'S AFFECTION

As mandarins, Lưu Bình and Dương Lễ are part of a long tradition that Vietnam inherited from China. Court and other government officials were appointed by the king, who selected them in competitive examinations held every three years in the capital. Ancient China and Vietnam were thus the first countries to have a "selective civil service" and one of the few places where a poor man with ability and ambition could rise to public office, sometimes even to become the king's son-in-law and successor. The mandarin's rank was shown by the style of his cap. Court officials wore caps with appendages shaped like a dragonfly's wings attached to each side.

119

THE OGRE'S VICTIM

The story of Thạch Sanh and Lý Thông is one of the few Vietnamese tales with a hero-overcoming-monster motif. Scholars believe that its unique features point to India as its origin, rather than China, the source of so many other Vietnamese legends.

Traditional Vietnamese instruments, except for the bamboo flute and the percussion instruments, fall chiefly into the string family. What to call Thạch Sanh's instrument was a matter to which I gave considerable thought. Though the pictures I have seen show him playing what looks like a *tỳ-bà* (variously defined as a two-stringed guitar or a pear-shaped lute), the text calls it simply *đàn,* meaning "stringed instrument." I chose *guitar* as the most generic term we have. Although in strict usage the word *guitar* refers to a specific instrument, it is, like its cousin *zither*, descended from the Greek *kithára*, a comprehensive word that meant lyre or lute.

TEARS OF PEARL

Châu Nương is a sea fairy and maid of the daughter of the Dragon King of the Waters. Her appeal to the goddess Quan Âm for help represents the joining of two originally distinct strands in Chinese-Vietnamese tradition: Taoism and Buddhism. Most of the stories that feature a fairy as heroine originated in the Taoist traditions of ancient China. The Taoists envisioned a world of fairies that encompassed every part of the universe: sky, mountains, forests, seas, lakes, and rivers.

The Dragon King of the Waters (Hải Long Vương) who lived in the Crystal Palace (Thủy-Tinh Cung) at the bottom of the sea, ruled the seas and all the water creatures. He had the form of a dragon, but could assume human form whenever he wished.

Fairies, who could be recognized by the long sash draped around their shoulders, often visited humans, usually to help some needy and deserving mortal; but they were forbidden by the celestial laws from becoming romantically involved with humans or entangled in their lives. There are many stories that relate the consequences that follow the breaking of this ban.

Orthodox Buddhism recognized no fairy world; instead, persons who attained perfection became Enlightened Ones or Buddhas. After they died,

those Enlightened Ones whose renunciation of self and of worldly pleasures resulted in service to others were worshipped as gods. Such a one is Quan Âm, the goddess of mercy and protectress of children, worshipped throughout Asia: in China as Kuanyin, in Japan as Kwannon, and in Korea as Kwanseium.

The mandarin ducks in Vạn Châu's embroidery are brightly colored birds with crested heads, much loved in Asia for their beauty. A pair of mandarin ducks symbolizes a happy husband and wife.

THIRD DAUGHTER

The names of Third Daughter and her sisters, First Daughter and Second Daughter, represent a custom still practiced by some families in Vietnam today, that of naming a child by his or her position in the family.

Vietnamese usually have three names. The family name stands first, followed by the middle, with the given name at the end. Some Vietnamese, including several traditional characters such as Lưu Bình and Dương Lễ, have only a family name and a given name. These characters are always referred to by their full name. Others, like people in real life, may be called by only their given names. Often the middle and first name are used together as a compound name, as is often done in the American South.

In modern-day Vietnam, the family name is never used alone or with such titles as Mr. or Ms. These are used only with the full name or with the given name. In legends, however, male and female heads of a family are often referred to by their family name. I have, therefore, followed this tradition in calling Third Daughter's mother Mrs. Lưu.

SECOND IN COMMAND

When Mộc Lan answers the commander's marriage proposal by saying that she has to get her parents' consent, she is not merely stalling. For a marriage to be legal in old Vietnam, the parents' consent was a necessity. Seldom, however, did the interested parties speak to each other directly, as does the commander to Mộc Lan. The boy's parents would hire a matchmaker to visit the girl's family and present their proposal, which included a recitation of the young man's excellent qualities, though sometimes a girl's family would take the initiative.

If the negotiations were successful, the families, and eventually the young couple, would meet. Gifts would be exchanged, and the boy and his family would come to the girl's home for a betrothal dinner. From the time of the betrothal, the contract, whether or not it was in written form, was considered binding, and the young people were accepted as full members of each other's families. The Vietnamese referred to the marriage relationship as a "hundred-year friendship" and to their spouse as their "hundred-year friend" (*bạn trăm năm*).

THE GOLDEN CARP

The most important holiday of the Vietnamese year is the one celebrated by Minh Chí and Kim Nương: New Year, called Tết ("the Festival") marks the beginning of spring in Vietnam—the first week of the first lunar month (in late January or early February by the Western calendar). It is a time for feasting and family reunion, a time to exchange gifts and cards, to wear new clothes, and to set off firecrackers.

But the most colorful part of the New Year festivities is the unicorn dance. Unicorns, like dragons, bring good fortune, and parades are held in their honor. The dance that serves as the climax of the parade is performed by two men dressed to represent the unicorn. One supplies the front legs and supports the head, a bearded, one-horned, many-colored mask. The other forms the body and back legs. After preliminary stunts and mock fights by acrobats, the unicorn dances. In order to receive the unicorn's blessing, and thus good fortune in the coming year, families hang money wrapped in red paper from rooftops or upper-story windows as an offering. The unicorn retrieves it by the "head" man climbing onto the shoulders of the man supporting the body. Everyone cheers when the unicorn at last snatches the money between his jaws and "eats" it.

PRONUNCIATION OF VIETNAMESE NAMES

The Vietnamese language has six tones represented by marks placed over or under the vowels:

1. The middle tone carries no mark. It has the pitch of a word at the beginning of an English sentence.

2. The low tone carries a grave accent (`). It has the pitch of a word at the end of an ordinary statement.

3. The high tone carries an acute accent (´). It has the pitch of a word at the end of an English question.

4 and 5. The two rising tones (? and ~) are pronounced the same by southern Vietnamese. The pitch starts a little below midlevel and glides upward to slightly above midlevel. Northern speakers make a distinction between these two tones.

6. The low rising tone carries a dot (.) under the vowel. The pitch starts lower than the low tone and rises slightly, with a staccato effect.

Other marks that are place over vowels (˘ and ˆ) or are attached to vowels (') change the sound or length of the vowel.

The pitch of the tones can be illustrated by the following sentences pronounced in normal conversational English:

Are you gỏing? Nó? Ọh! Then hurrỳ.

In English, intonation reveals the speaker's emotions or intent, whereas in Vietnamese a change of pitch changes the meaning of the word. This can be seen from the following examples:

bao – bag

bào – make smooth

báo – newspaper

bạo – cruel

bảo – precious

bão – storm

Pronounce *ng* as in *singer; igh* as in *high; ow* as in *how;* o̅o̅ as in *too;* ŏŏ as in *took; u* as in *sun* or *sung.*

Vietnamese *t* is unaspirated (as in *little* or *stop*); *th* is aspirated (as in *table).* Final consonants are "swallowed," instead of being "spit out" as in English. The barred *d* (đ) is pronounced like English *d*; the unbarred *d* (d) is pronounced like *z* by Northern speakers and like the *y* in *yes* by Southern speakers.

- Bao Công (bow come)

- Cảnh Sinh (cah-on shin)

- Châu Long (chah-o͞o lum): Pearl Dragon

- Châu Nương (chah-o͞o no͞o-ung): Pearl Lady

- Dương Lễ (yo͞o-ung lay-ay)

- đàn (dahn): stringed instrument

- Hải Long Vương (high-igh lum vo͞o-ung): Sea Dragon King

- Hoa (hwah)

- Huỳnh Nga (hwin ngah): Yellow Moon

- Kim Nương (keem no͞o-ung): Golden Lady

- Lão Ba (low-ow bah): Old-man Three

- Lương (lo͞o-ung)

- Lưu Bình (lo͞o-o͞o bin)

- Lý Quang (lee quahng); Lý Thông (lee towm)

- Minh Chí (min chee): Bright Ambition; Minh Long (min lum): Bright Dragon

- Mộc Lan (mowp lahn): Magnolia (literally, "Wood Orchid")

- Quan Âm (quahn um)

- Thạch Sanh (taht shahn)

- Thanh Tùng (tahn to͞om): Green Pine

- Thủy-Tinh Cung (twee-ee tin co͞om): Crystal Palace

- Trần (trun)

- Vạn Châu (von chah-o͞o): Ten thousand Pearls or Ten thousand Tears

- Văn Lương (von lo͞o-ung)

- Việt-Nam (vee-et nahm): Vietnam

128

Proctor Free Library
Proctor, Vermont

1. Books may be kept two weeks and may be renewed once for the same period, except 7 day books and magazines.

2. A fine is charged for each day a book is not returned according to the above rule. No book will be issued to any person incurring such a fine until it has been paid.

3. All injuries to books beyond reasonable wear and all losses shall be made good to the satisfaction of the Librarian.

Each borrower is held responsible for all books charged on his card and for all fines accruing on the same.

GAYLORD
R